# TO: ASPEN

Lizzie ♡

xo,
nj gray

N.J. GRAY

Visit my website at www.authornjgray.com
Cover Designer: Murphy Rae, www.murphyrae.com
Editor and Interior Designer: Jovana Shirley,
Unforeseen Editing, www.unforeseenediting.com



This book is a work of fiction. Names, characters, places, and incidents either are products of the author's imagination or are used fictitiously. Any resemblance to actual persons, living or dead, events, or locales is entirely coincidental.

ISBN-13: 9798356294716

*For Korra, my best girl.*

# 1

# A FROSTY WELCOME

My grip on the steering wheel tightens as I brace myself for sudden death at any moment. I'm used to the snow and the cold. Winters are brutal where I grew up. Hell, the winters at Columbia University the last three years weren't kind to me either. But up here, making one small move on the side of a mountain could be the end for me.

My flight didn't get in until nine, so I haven't seen the vast wonderland of one of Colorado's most luxurious ski towns. I can barely see the road in front of me. After a two-hour delay in New York, a near four-hour flight, a three-hour layover in Denver, and another hour connection to Aspen, I'm done with traveling for a while. Luckily, I have two weeks before classes start back up, and I get to do this all over again on my return flight.

Turning down another dark, snow-covered road, I can almost hear my pulse hammering in my chest. The directions on the dash tell me to turn right, but all I see is a snowbank twice as tall as my rental car.

Suddenly, blaring chimes fill the silence in the car, and I squeak in surprise. I grab my phone out of the cupholder and slide my thumb across the screen.

"Henry?" I answer, waiting for the warmth of my friend's voice to greet me.

"Hey, Aspen. You finding your way all right?"

I throw my head back against the headrest in frustration, releasing an audible sigh.

"I take that as a no?" He laughs. "I told you, you should've flown in with me yesterday. Then, you wouldn't be driving in the dark."

I stubbornly refused his free first-class ticket out here when he invited me. Just because Henry is a rich trust-fund baby doesn't mean I feel any more comfortable taking his handouts. That's not how I was raised. My parents' income didn't include the extra zeros like Henry's and his friends' parents have. I can never shake the idea that other people's money comes with strings even though I know Henry would never use it for manipulation. Staying at his family's cabin for winter break still fills me with this uncomfortable guilt of not being able to return the favor, but I'm glad I don't have to spend Christmas in my dorm. Besides, Henry is more like family to me now anyway.

"Where are you?" he asks.

"GPS is telling me I've arrived, but unless your cabin is a giant bunker of snow, I think I'm lost."

"Shit. I forgot the plows were out earlier today. They must've blocked the main driveway. Keep going up around the hill. Take your next right and then the right after that. That'll bring you in the back way. It should be cleared."

"Well, I didn't bring my snowshoes if it's not."

He chuckles. "I'll come out there and rescue you on my skis if I have to."

I turn the car ninety degrees to continue where he directed me. After I pass over the hill, warm twinkly lights covering dozens of trees begin to lead me up a driveway to a … *house*?

This is *so* not a house. This place should be pictured on the front cover of *Luxury Home Magazine*, Christmas edition. Either that or in some Hallmark movie.

"Um … Henry?"

"What is it? Are you okay?"

"I knew your family wasn't going to have a quaint little log cabin in the woods but *come on*. This is just showing off."

"Aye, I see you!" he says eagerly. "I'll be right out."

As I shove my phone into my coat pocket, I scan the "cabin" in front of me with my mouth pretty much in my lap.

The door opens, and Henry jogs toward my car in a thick knit sweater and winter boots with untied laces.

"I'm so glad you made it," he says as I climb out, quickly wrapping his arms around me. "Go and get out of the cold. I'll grab your bags."

"Oh, it's just the one for me."

I pull my duffel from the passenger seat, and he quickly takes it.

"You pack light." Henry swings it over his shoulder.

The wind picks up, and I squeeze my arms tightly in front of me, trying to trap my heat.

"Come on, come on. It's freezing out here!"

I can hear my boots shifting and compacting the snow under each footstep to the front door. The sound is amplified in the silence of a snow-covered forest. "It's so peaceful and quiet up here."

"Just wait until you get one of Jesse's drinks in your hand. You'll never want to leave." Henry holds the door and gestures me inside.

The warmth of the house quickly surrounds me. The smell of pine and hot apple toddies hits my nose in an inviting way, but the news Henry just softballed me hits me harder, and I hesitate in the doorway.

"Wait. Jesse? I thought it was just you, me, and your sister?"

An innocent smile creeps onto his face—one I know all too well. He's trying to lessen the blow of whatever he is going to tell me next.

"Henry?" I ask, noticing almost half a dozen shoes in the entryway.

"Clara decided to join our parents in Paris for Christmas this year. I know; I was just as surprised as you are." His face pinches with unease as I cross my arms. "Luke's dad had some work to finish up in Japan, so he was going to be all alone. I invited him … out of the goodness of my heart! And then he invited Jesse …"

I work my jaw and wait, knowing there is more.

"And Jesse invited Baylor," he mumbles under his breath as if I won't hear him.

"Baylor is here?" I whisper in a hushed tone.

Henry winces. "What was I supposed to do?"

"Tell him to fuck off! Duh! He can afford a ticket to anywhere he wants in the world. Why does he have to be *here*?"

Baylor Frost, Henry's oldest—and most infuriating—friend, is the last person I want to spend my Christmas with.

"I talked to him. He said he will be on his best behavior."

"Oh, he said that, did he?" I arch a brow.

He tilts his head slightly. "Well, he said he'd do his best."

"Satan has better manners than that guy. Why didn't you tell me he was going to be here?"

"Because you wouldn't have come."

"Damn right!" I toss my hair out of my face in frustration. "You know what? I'm okay with you buying my plane ticket out of here after withholding this from me. The nerve!"

Henry blocks the door. "Yeah? Would you rather be back at your drafty dorm with no one around? Or would you like a ticket to frigid Minnesota to spend the holidays with your fucked up parents and listen to them fight the whole time?"

I step closer to him and narrow my eyes. "I would rather be in a fish tank full of piranhas than be stuck in a house with Baylor for two weeks. *Move.*"

Henry steps aside, his shoulders sinking.

As I thrust the door back open, I'm met with thick snowflakes being thrown at me from high winds. "Where did this come from?" I look up at the sky and get pelted with more frozen fluffballs.

"Welcome to Colorado." He leans against the doorframe. "This is just the start of it. We're supposed to get several inches throughout the night. There's no way you're driving back down the mountain in this."

"Oh, yes, I am." I zip my jacket up as high as it goes and continue toward my car.

Snow is quickly covering the windshield.

Henry lets out a loud sigh. "Aspen, he already knows you're here. If you leave now, he'll win."

I stop mid-step. If there's one thing Henry knows about me, it's that I hate losing. I don't back down. Ever. Especially when it comes to Baylor fucking Frost.

I release a growl that could compete with some of the predators I know are lurking out there and stomp back inside. "That was low. Even for you."

"It worked, didn't it?" Henry shakes his head. "This will be fun. I promise."

"Don't promise things you have no control over."

"You're right. But if there's one thing—one person—who can control Baylor, it's you."

I choke out a laugh. "Me?"

"You're the only one who can stand an argument with him long enough to see it through. Everyone always gives up or gives in. Everyone but you. I think he secretly likes having you around because of that."

"Yeah, right. He can't stand me. He's told me several times. And not in such delicate words," I deadpan.

"Maybe after two weeks, you two will get sick of this stupid rivalry thing you've got going on."

"Or one of us will kill the other. Can you at least tell me where the weapons are in the house? I'd like to be prepared."

"Aspen," Henry scolds me.

"What? When I finally drive a stake through his cold heart, you can tell the jury it was in self-defense." I lower my voice and say, "It'll be our little secret."

"Do you think my family is a bunch of vampire hunters, hiding wooden stakes in vaults around the house?"

I shrug. "I'll take a bow and arrow. Don't they hunt elk out here?"

"You're ridiculous." He grins and bats the snowflakes off the pom of my hat.

I wipe away the ones that melted on my face. My bare and plain face.

I'm suddenly aware of just how *plain* I look. From head to toe, I am a mess and in no way ready to face Henry's friends. Most of the ones I've met are pretty okay—sans Baylor—but I am always prepared when I know I am going to be around them. I am the only one in Henry's close-knit group that doesn't have a seven- or eight-figure inheritance. I actually don't have much more than three figures in my bank account right now, and it feels like that number is just floating above my head in a giant neon sign for all of them to see.

There is a certain *je ne sais quoi* that comes with having as much money as they do. A finesse I could never capture. I know it isn't their fault that their parents are wealthy or that they've never really had to work for anything. But when you're around people with that much power, that much confidence and ignorance, you have to be able to hold your own.

I swear Baylor can smell people who don't come from money. That's why he sticks his nose up at me so often. I don't fart Chanel perfume or fan myself with hundred-dollar bills, so naturally, I'm inferior.

Henry is different. We might've come from opposite worlds, but he always does well with blurring them together.

"You want to come say hi to the guys? Jesse and Luke are still playing pool in the basement, but I'm sure Jesse will be willing to take a break to fix you a stiff one."

"As tempting as that is, I think I'd like to go take a shower and try to get some sleep. It's been a long day, and I have airplane all over me."

He tilts his head as he takes my coat. "Don't hide, Aspen."

"I'm not!"

"You know what they do if they think they've scared you off." His eyes fill with warning. "They come hunting."

"They? Like you aren't one of them?" I laugh, struggling out of my winter boots.

His friends might be intimidating, but they don't scare me.

"That hurts." Henry holds his hand over his heart, feigning insult. "Maybe you should get some sleep. You're crabby."

"I'm sorry. I'm just readying myself for two weeks of drunken, rich asshats with raging testosterone and no filters. No offense."

"You're going to be just fine. They can use someone like you to keep their egos in check." His smile eases my nerves.

I roll my eyes and move toward the winding staircase with a giant fifteen-foot Christmas tree in the middle of it. "Do I just pick a room?"

"Oh, here, I can show you around."

"I'm sure I can figure it out." I stop him.

Henry laughs and shakes his head. He's used to my stubbornness, and he knows when I'm not in the mood to be around anyone. I'm pretty sure his sister is to thank for that.

"The first room on the left is mine. All the bedrooms have a small wreath on the door. Just pick one that doesn't look occupied."

I raise a brow and curl my lip. "Am I going to find—"

"Everyone is down in the pool room. Don't worry." He gives me a wide, knowing grin.

Let's just say there was a time I walked in on Jesse, Luke, and a sexy little cowgirl at a Halloween party. If I could burn the images out of my head, I would.

I nod as Henry shoves his hands into his pockets and turns, but I bolt down the stairs and wrap my arms around his neck before he can get too far.

"Whoa, what's this for?"

I squeeze him until his arms wrap around my middle. "I would've really felt alone if I'd stayed back at my dorm. Thank you."

His arms flex tighter at my words. "Don't mention it, Pen. I'm glad you're here."

I feel his lips against the top of my head before I let go and head up to find a bed and a shower. I pass five bedrooms, eyeing the one at the end of the hallway and hoping one of the boys hasn't claimed it. I want as much privacy as I can get.

I knock and slowly open the door, releasing a breath of relief when I see the king-size bed is still made and there are no bags or luggage in sight.

The pine headboard and armoire add to the cozy cabin aesthetic along with the cashmere plaid throw blanket and the fluffy duvet. It pains me to turn away from what I know will be a deep slumber, but I will regret going to sleep in my filth if I don't bathe now.

I squeal to myself when I walk into my very own bathroom. The Jacuzzi tub will have to be a nightly ritual while I'm here with its view of the mountainside and small twinkling lights from town. But tonight, the shower is calling my name.

My head is too busy, trying to restructure the Christmas I thought I was going to have with the one I'm stuck with instead, that I forget to grab my shower supplies from my duffel. Luckily, there's some body wash, shampoo, and conditioner already in the shower. It's expensive-looking, so I only use a little dollop of each before I shut the water off and wring my hair out.

*Towels, towels. Where are the towels?*

I frantically look around as the steam begins to dissipate and my skin puckers with tiny goose bumps.

With no towels in sight, I make my way to the armoire I remember seeing just outside the bathroom, but as soon as I open the door, I'm greeted with a collared black shirt, covering a hard chest.

A cry tears through my throat in surprise. I quickly look up, and my gaze lands on two familiar dark green eyes.

Baylor.

He tilts his head, and strands of brown hair fall across his brow. "What are you doing in my room, *Penny*?"

# 2

# FIND A PENNY

Every fiber in my body tells me to cover myself. To hide my soft flesh from him. He doesn't deserve to see it.

But I don't flinch. I keep myself steady. Confident. He expects me to squirm underneath his stare, but I won't give him the satisfaction.

Baylor's eyes remain on mine rather than running down my naked body, and I think that's more of an insult than his next words.

"The *help* stay downstairs, Penny."

As his nickname for me falls from his mouth again, I do my best not to shake at the feeling it always leaves behind, like tiny insects are crawling on my skin.

Penny. *Ugh.*

He got the brilliant idea to call me that shortly after Henry began calling me Pen, and it is not as cute or endearing as it sounds.

Pen is short for Aspen. It's simple. Convenient. Respectful.

Penny is just another one of Baylor's fun ways of shoving my lack of fortune in my face. Penniless doesn't exactly roll off the tongue like Penny does. A penny would never be found in his possession. Not even beneath the wads of large bills he keeps in his deep pockets. It's nothing to him. Just a worthless piece of currency. A dull coin beneath his shoe on the sidewalk, not even worth picking up for a bit of luck.

But for as small and insignificant as I am, he sure enjoys stepping on me every chance he gets.

I narrow my eyes up at him, trying not to shiver as water from my hair drips down my back. "Fuck you, Baylor. Get out."

A smile pulls at his lips. "I believe you're the lost one here. I know Henry well enough to know he didn't send you up here for me. He usually buys me more expensive girls."

I take a slow breath so I don't pummel him to death. Henry has never bought his women. None of them would have to. For some strange reason, women seem to simply fall at Baylor's feet. I mean, sure, he's good-looking, but he's a narcissistic asshole with a God complex. There's nothing attractive about that.

"I was clearly here first. Find another room."

"Some of us don't just throw our clothes on the ground and dig them out of a giant garbage bag during vacation." He gestures to my black duffel lying on the floor behind him.

"Mine were hung up in the closet before you got here. Besides, this room is the farthest away from everyone and—"

He suddenly stops, and my heart dances in my chest. Baylor leans down and takes a strand of my blonde hair between his long fingers. He steps closer, inhales, and releases a low growl that heats my skin. As much as I don't like it, I almost beg him to do it again.

"You used my shampoo."

"I …" I fumble for words as he continues to twirl my hair in his grasp, but I quickly find my tongue again and grin. "I did. And your conditioner too."

Baylor drops my hair and rubs his fingers together like they're dirty. "Not exactly the way I usually leave my scent on a woman."

I snarl in disgust. "Get a good whiff because it's the only scent of yours I'll ever wear."

A tremor courses up my body when I feel something hard begin to press on my stomach. I fight the urge to look down, but I can't help myself.

*Is he really …*

My eyes slowly trail down the front of his collared black button-up that practically melts to his perfectly trimmed body. All of his clothes are tailored, so it comes as no surprise, but the sight still makes my mouth dry. My gaze dips lower to the waist of his black trousers, which does little to hide his growing erection.

My breath hitches, and I quickly look back up at him, but his eyes must've lowered when mine did and are still stuck where they landed.

Warmth swiftly replaces my chilled skin, trailing down to my core. My thighs start to ache, and my breasts swell from the attention they're getting. I hate that my body is betraying me at a time like this, but it can only be because I haven't been naked around a man in over a year. There's no way Baylor Frost, of all men, is turning me on with just a look.

Baylor's tongue peeks out, sweeping over his bottom lip before his deep emerald eyes flick back up to mine. "Get your clothes and get out. Now." The roughness in his voice gives him away. I'm affecting him and not in a way he's used to.

Baylor's never seen me without clothes. This is an entirely new ball game, and the thrill of making him uncomfortable excites me too much to back down. Maybe I'm more like Henry's friends than I thought.

I shake away that idea and put my hands to work.

"I don't want to go," I whisper, dragging my hands up and over the curve of my hips toward my waist.

I walk my fingers inward and trace the delicate skin beneath my breasts, watching the notch in his throat bob as he tries to swallow. His eyes grow darker as his pupils dilate.

"What do you think you're doing?" he rasps, watching my movements with an intensity that motivates me.

"Just trying to get warm—that's all." I question my morals and how far I'm willing to take this when my fingers gently tug on my hardened nipples. My head drops back at the sudden arousal shooting through me from my own touch, but I keep my eyes trained on him.

If I make him uncomfortable enough, he'll have to leave. *Right?*

My questionable theory crumbles when Baylor goes from watching my meticulous fingers to pushing his body against mine.

He takes three giant steps forward, keeping me steady with a widespread hand on my lower back as he forces me farther into the bathroom.

My eyes go wide as my ass hits the vanity with a thud. I grunt or moan—too surprised to hear the difference. My lips parting with such an erotic sound makes Baylor's gaze fall to them, as if I commanded them to.

His warm palm twitches like he wants to slide his hands down and hoist me up onto the counter. Instead, he hastily removes it and shoves a finger in my face. "You have no idea what you're messing with, Penny. Careful."

My chest heaves against his as my heart rattles around in my rib cage like a butterfly trying to escape its prison. I don't know what I was expecting when I decided to play his game but I wasn't ready for this overwhelming feeling of fear and … desire.

*Desire?*

I deny it the moment I recognize the feeling, but I can't ignore the dampness between my legs.

Baylor's mouth comes an inch closer to mine, but as soon as my hands connect with his chest, his equally hungry stare is replaced with the cold steel I know all too well.

*What the hell just happened?*

"I'll give you the room," he finally says, lowering his mouth so I can feel his breath against my neck, "as long as you promise me you'll never do that again. Not for me or anyone else in this house. You hear me?"

All I manage is a single nod in agreement.

Baylor's hand rifles in his front pocket, and he pulls out a few large bills, throwing a dark grin down at me as he shoves the money in my face. "For the show."

My blood boils. I slide one of my legs between his and slowly raise my knee to his groin. "Put that back in your pocket, or I'll make sure you never have children."

Baylor's brows shoot up as the threat drips from my tongue. He chuckles, placing the money back inside his pants. Then, he leaves me, walking out with a certain swagger in his step I'm sure all the boys mastered at a douchebag academy of some sort.

"I'll come by in the morning to grab my things. *Do not* touch anything," I hear him say from the bedroom door before it slams shut.

I hold on to the sink for a few minutes until I can gather myself again, and then I saunter over to the closet. The wood door slides open with the tiniest bit of effort, revealing Baylor's neatly organized wardrobe. I run my fingers over the expensive fabric of his shirts and menacingly take one out, slip it over my head, and climb into bed.

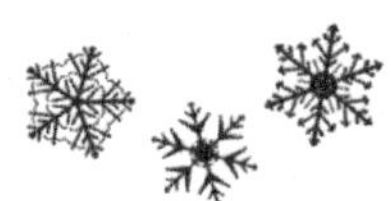

His scent invades my nose and alarms me from my sleep in the early hours of the morning. Baylor's clean, sweet smell of bergamot and persimmon from his shampoo and the airy, woodsy smell on his shirt give me the illusion of what it must be like to be wrapped in his arms. It confuses me why that doesn't make me want to rip the shirt off and chop my hair with the nearest pair of scissors, but I ignore the lack of disgust and focus on my grumbling stomach.

I stand and look down at the white cuffs of the button-up I'm swimming in and smile. The fabric is soft and luxurious, but, fortunately, prone to wrinkles. I giggle as I remove it and carefully place it back on the hanger in the closet, precisely where I found it.

After changing into jeans and a dark green flannel, I fix my hair into some loose curls and put on a spot of makeup before heading downstairs to find some breakfast.

I'm led to the kitchen by strings of frosted garland and warm lights. I wish I could frame the view of the snow-covered pine trees and mountain peaks from the large bay window. It almost doesn't look real. I don't understand how Mr. and Mrs. Donner miss this every year to spend the holiday in Paris. There's no way the view there is as good as this one.

I'm surprised to find I'm not alone with how quiet the house is when I meet one of the Donner family's workers, Marta, taking ingredients out of the refrigerator. She looks exhausted and crabby, but I would be too if I had to get up this early every morning to feed a bunch of people. I guess that's what I'm doing, but I got plenty of sleep last night, and I want to make breakfast even though I don't have to.

It takes a lot of convincing, but I finally pry the eggs out of her grip and send her back to bed.

My stomach growls as I familiarize myself with the kitchen, searching for ingredients, bowls, and a pan. I've never made food for four guys, so I decide on pancakes since they're filling and easy to make a lot of.

"Aspen Holly." A deep voice pierces through the quiet.

I jump, sending my bowl onto the floor. I quickly turn and see Luke wincing at the loud crash of metal.

"Jesus, Luke! Are you trying to give me a heart attack?" I try to calm my racing pulse.

"Sorry about that. Good thing it was empty, eh?" he says, handing it back to me. "I heard you got in last night. How come you didn't come hang out with us?"

I smile to hide my nerves. "I was just tired."

"We didn't scare you away by crashing your plans with Henry, did we?"

I shake my head. *Was I that obvious?* "Why are you awake so early?"

"I'm an early riser. It's a curse and a blessing, I guess."

"Why do you say that?"

"Well, I don't always get my beauty rest." His grin is flirtatious as he slides down the counter next to me. He braces the heels of his hands on the marble countertop behind him.

"And the blessing?" I dare to ask.

"Well, today, I get to spend some quiet time with you." His grin is the only thing I find attractive about him. That and his rather remarkable IQ.

The way he acts with Henry and his friends makes it seem like he's an ignorant twat, but the guy is kind of a genius. He's already completed his MBA to satisfy his father's wishes, but he's still taking classes to get his master's in political science. I would never date the guy, but I might trust him to run this country someday.

He lowers his chin in an attempt to catch my gaze, but I don't fall for it. "What are you making me?"

"I'm making *everyone* pancakes," I tell him. "Hungry?"

"Starved." I notice the playfulness in his voice and feel his eyes studying me as I begin combining all the dry ingredients together.

Luke is a flirt, and it gets him into trouble more often than not. Especially when it comes to a select few female professors. He's the kind of guy who always wants the girl he can't have. Relentless little fuck, if you ask me. Usually, he leaves me be when Henry's around, but he's taking advantage of his time alone with me. He should know by now that it's a wasted effort.

"Mmm, blueberries. My favorite." Luke plucks a few berries out of the container next to me. "I just love the way the juice explodes on my tongue when I pop one open in my mouth."

I shudder, trying to ignore how he's now pressed into my side. He has a way with words—I'll give him that.

"Have some with me, Aspen." He reaches his hand up and grazes a blueberry along my bottom lip.

My eyes flit up to meet his as I slowly open my mouth and take his offering.

"My God." His eyes heat as his thumb brushes the soft pink skin. "Your lips are so sof—"

Henry rounds the corner, and relief washes over me. "I heard a crash."

Luke breaks away, but not before Henry notices.

"Aye! Come on, Luke! What did I say about her?"

I take a deep breath to regain my sanity.

"Yeah, yeah. She's off-limits. I was only having a bit of fun." Luke rolls his eyes and laughs to himself, settling into a chair. "You should really learn to share your toys, Donner."

Henry darts his eyes over to his friend with a look that could kill. "Sorry about him, Pen. He's a horny prick sometimes."

"Only sometimes?" I murmur.

Henry comes around the island and bumps his naked shoulder against mine. A pair of buffalo plaid pajama bottoms hang low on his waistline, and as many times as I've seen him without a shirt, I still get impressed by his tightly trimmed abdomen. Whatever secret society these boys are a part of, having washboard abs and a well-sculpted face must have been a requirement. Each of them looks like a Greek god businessman you know you shouldn't go near unless you are looking to get your heart broken. Fortunately for them, they find a lot of girls begging for the thrill of being in their presence even if it's just for one night.

I am the anomaly, I guess. I think I've seen them use their lines and tricks on women too many times to find them attractive.

Luke cocks his head at me as he tosses back the rest of the blueberries in his hand.

I narrow my eyes briefly before a thundering voice rumbles throughout the house.

"ASPEN!" My name echoes up to the tall wooden ceiling.

Henry freezes with a bag of coffee beans in hand and glances over his shoulder at me from the coffee press. "It hasn't even been a day yet. What could you possibly have done already?" he asks, catching the amused expression lighting up my face.

I don't have to guess to know the footsteps barreling down the stairs are Baylor's.

I ready myself with a smile I know will piss him off. "Good morning, sunshine," I say as he charges toward me, fisting the white shirt I wore to bed last night.

"You fucking brat! Why is my shirt all wrinkled?"

"Well, have you tried not strangling the thing to death?" I glance down at his hand gripping the shirt.

He practically shakes at my response. "I'd like it better if it were your throat!"

Heat rolls down my stomach, and I swallow as unwelcome images press their way into my thoughts.

"What is wrong with you?" Baylor's dark brows furrow.

I back up when he takes a step forward, giving me a flashback of last night's events in my head. Even though I'm fully clothed now, I feel like all he can see is my naked body when he looks at me.

Henry steps between us and pushes on his friend's chest. "You said you were going to be nice."

"Me?" Baylor roars and throws a hand in the air at me. "She's the one who stole my room last night and touched my stuff!"

"Why is it that every time Aspen is around, you turn into a child, Baylor?" Henry shakes his head and looks between the two of us. "Can't you two play nice for a change? C'mon. It's Christmas."

"I don't know what you're talking about. I'm being super jolly and making breakfast for everyone." I bite my lip to hide a teasing grin.

"Blueberries in mine, please," Luke shouts.

"Pancakes?" Baylor scoffs. "I'm not eating that shit."

"And why not?" Henry frowns, stepping away to pour coffee grinds into the coffeemaker.

"Well, besides the fact that she'll probably poison mine—"

I shrug, letting him know it's crossed my mind.

"I don't eat that crap." He pats his hard stomach. I can see the ripples in his abdomen through his thin white T-shirt.

I make sure he sees my eye roll before I pin him with a glare.

"What the hell is happening down here?" Jesse shuffles into the kitchen in an open robe, boxer briefs, and fuzzy slippers. He rubs the sleep from his eyes.

Even with slept-on hair and a crease from his pillow marking his cheek, he still looks like he could work a runway. And rightfully so. Both of Jesse Cane's mothers own a luxury clothing company that is featured in New York *and* Paris Fashion Week every year. His style is always on point, even when he's just rolled out of bed.

"Morning, Jesse." I nod over Baylor's shoulder.

"Ah, that explains it. You two are in the same room together," Jesse says, nodding toward me and Baylor. "Why don't you two just fuck and get it over with? It'll make things so much easier."

Baylor glances down at my lips just before I curl them in disgust.

"Something tells me she'd be just as boring and stiff in bed as she is like this." Baylor gestures to all of me, making me narrow my eyes into thin slits. "Although maybe he's right, Penny. A good fucking could do you some good."

My cheeks redden like embers of the hottest coals. "A good fucking, huh?"

Baylor's lips twitch as he nods.

I take a step forward and trail a gentle finger down his chest. "And who would volunteer for such an exhausting task?"

Out of the corner of my eye, I see Luke shoot his hand into the air as he chokes on some blueberries.

"Because someone as *stiff* as me"—I quickly glance down at the seam of Baylor's joggers—"would need an equally stiff partner. It would be quite the workout." I bat my eyes back up at him. My chest barely touches his now.

Baylor straightens himself, trying to make me feel smaller.

I stare up into his dark eyes, unafraid. "There's no way you could satisfy me. Not in this lifetime or any other."

Baylor's voice lowers to almost a whisper. "I saw the way I affected you last night without even touching you. You'd be surprised with just how fast I could satisfy you if you wanted me to."

Someone in the room clears their throat.

My shallow breathing fills the sudden silence in the kitchen, making me aware of how all four men are staring at me.

Henry's hand circles my wrist, pulling me away from Baylor in haste. Jesse shoots me a dark grin as I pass him on the way out of the kitchen. When we reach the living room, Henry releases me, his jaw firm.

"Jesus. What?" I ask.

"What did he mean about last night? I thought you went straight to bed?"

"I did! I didn't know it was *his* room. He surprised me when I got out of the shower and made it weird." My shoulders sag as I let out a long sigh.

"Weird? Weird how?"

"Well, he saw me naked!" I blush.

Henry's brown eyes widen with surprise. The muscles in his jaw tic away as he fights the urge to act as the overprotective big brother. "If he so much as laid a hand on you—"

"Relax. I got him to leave without much effort." I raise my chin pridefully.

Curiosity trims Henry's features, but eventually, he shrugs and smiles. "You really know how to get him going. Just be careful, Pen. You don't know Baylor like I do."

My lips stretch into a smile. "I found the kitchen knives earlier. I'll be just fine."

Henry slides a hand down his face as I leave him to finish making breakfast.

# 3

# OH, WHAT FUN

I almost bite Henry's arm off when he shakes me awake the next morning. The sun hasn't even risen over the peaks of the mountains yet, but with the fresh snow we got last night, the boys want to make sure they get on the slopes before everyone else.

"Fresh powder makes for the best skiing," Henry explains.

Yeah, okay. But a proper eight hours of sleep makes for the best *Aspen.*

Jesse has the audacity to ask for another pancake breakfast as I trudge my way down the stairs in yoga pants and a Columbia University sweatshirt. I answer him with a middle finger and a furrowed brow that only make him and the others laugh.

I made the mistake of telling everyone I had experience snowboarding during dinner last night. Not a total lie, but far from the truth. One of my sixth-grade field trips was to Ski Hill near my hometown—Minnesota isn't exactly known for its mountains unless you count Duluth's steep roads that feel like you're driving vertically up a cliff—so I don't know if that counts as experience in snowboarding, considering I spent more time on my butt than I did on my board. But that didn't make me shy away from telling Henry and his friends I was practically an Olympic athlete. Now, I am trading that tiny hill in my hometown for an eleven-thousand-foot mountain without touching a board in over ten years.

All because of Baylor.

He made a huge deal, saying I was going to be a burden to everyone on the slopes because I had the least amount of experience. So … I might've embellished my skills a bit. I can't help it. Baylor ignites something inside me I can't control. When I'm around him, my mouth has a mind of its own.

My stomach twists at the thought of being strapped to a board at the top of a mountain. What if I accidentally go down the wrong side and just disappear forever?

Hey, that's not a bad idea. That could solve all my problems at the moment.

Henry sips on the contents in his thermos. The smell of his coffee makes me want to snuggle up by the fire with a giant, fuzzy blanket and a cup of my own.

"You brought more than that poor excuse for a coat you wore here, right?" he asks.

I yawn and rub my eyes. "What's wrong with my jacket?"

"That thing won't block the wind or keep you warm if you get wet up there."

Jesse, Luke, and Baylor hustle around me in variations of long underwear, gathering the rest of their winter gear.

"She doesn't even have proper base layers, man. I told you she has no idea what she's doing." Baylor shakes his head at me, slipping his arms through a zip-up and then a thick jacket.

"I do too! I'm just not a pussy like you when it comes to the cold." I cross my arms, already feeling goose bumps from Luke opening the garage door.

Henry chuckles and plops a hat over my head, shimmying it down so it's covering my ears completely.

I do my best to hold a scowl, but one can only look so tough with a big, fluffy pom on the top of their head.

"You've got snow pants, right?"

I nod.

"You should take my sister's jacket. You two are about the same size, and it will serve you better up there." Henry steps out into the garage, where the boys are loading up their skis.

I follow him and rub my arms when the warmth of the cabin is taken from me. Baylor sees me shiver and shakes his head at me, and I throw a scowl in his direction.

Henry rifles through a storage bin and takes out a thick white jacket, a helmet, and some goggles. "What size shoe are you?"

"Seven. Why?"

"Her boots might be a little big, but they should fit you. That way, you don't have to rent anything."

"I brought boots though."

"He means, snowboard boots." Baylor raises his brow. "C'mon, Henry. She's just going to hold us up. Leave her here."

"Why don't you go load the rest of your shit in the truck and leave her alone? If she says she's good, she's good." Henry nods, handing me Clara's jacket.

My stomach twists again at Henry's misplaced trust. "Thanks," I say, staring down at my feet.

I don't like lying to him, but I can't back out now—even if it is a death wish.

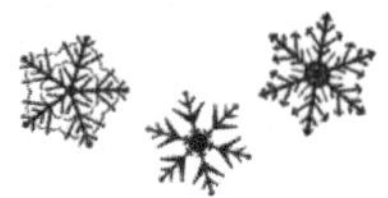

The sun begins to rise as we all load into the gondola lift, turning the sky into a beautiful lavender backdrop to a mountainous skyline.

I stare out the window just above Baylor's head and take it all in as we head up the mountainside. Out of the corner of my eye, I see him smile—no doubt finding my awed expression hilarious.

Jesse nudges my thigh with his ski pole before I can make a smart remark. "Pretty great, isn't it?"

My lips stretch into a giant grin. "I can't imagine anything more beautiful."

Baylor clears his throat before covering his face with his balaclava and goggles. I can't see his eyes, but I still glare into the red-tinted reflection of myself just the same.

I adjust my helmet as we near our stop, gripping my board with my gloves. My stomach starts to turn again as skiers and snowboarders make their way down the hill in front of me, spraying up the fresh snow as they decrease in speed. I watch carefully, trying to learn as much as I can from their movements while trying not to puke.

Henry, Jesse, and Luke grab their skis while Baylor and I follow them out into the brisk mountain air with our snowboards. My boot catches on a mound of snow I don't notice, and before I can get ready to eat snow, there's a sudden, forceful tug on my hood.

I look back as soon as my feet are underneath me again and watch, wide-eyed, as Baylor slowly uncurls a fistful of my jacket with a huff.

"Watch where you're going, will ya?"

I pinch my face as he stalks past me but still manage a small, "Thanks," while he's still in earshot.

"Aye, Pen!" Henry waves from up ahead. "Come check this out!"

I hurry to catch up, carefully watching where I'm walking this time. It's not until I reach his side that I look up. Henry slides an arm over my shoulders, and I'm grateful for the extra stability he gives me with it because the view nearly knocks me over.

"And all my parents get is the lousy Eiffel Tower." Henry laughs once, eyeing the sea of blanketed mountain peaks in front of us.

I'm speechless. I've never seen something that has literally taken my breath away, but it is like I'm frozen in time. A core memory, etching every detail, every color into a safe place in my mind. I feel small and insignificant but in the best way possible.

"Are you crying?"

And just like that, Baylor ruins a perfect moment.

Henry smiles and runs a gloved finger over the single tear before it can reach my chin. The rough texture of his glove only smears the wetness over more of my face, which the wind finds instantly.

Embarrassed and cold, I pull my scarf up higher and lower my goggles. The clear lens doesn't hide my eyes but saves my face from the bitter wind whirling around us.

"Last one to the bottom buys drinks tonight!" Luke shouts, pushing off with his skis.

Jesse quickly shuffles after him, digging his poles into the ground and bending his knees.

Henry drops his arm and nudges me, clicking his boots into his skis. "Let's go, Pen! I can cover you. These boys know how to raise a fuckin' tab."

"You go! I want to take this in a little longer before the sun is all the way up."

He slams his skis into the side of the hill, stopping a bit below me. "I'm not going to leave you up here."

I wave my hands at him. "I'll be right down! They've already got a big head start! Go, go!"

Henry hesitates another second before pushing off. I watch them all zigzag their way down the mountain until they disappear and then let out a sigh of relief.

"I knew it."

My head snaps to the sound of Baylor's voice. "For the love of—" I grind my teeth together. "Why are you still here?"

"I wanted to see for myself."

"See what?"

"How you're going to get yourself down this mountain."

I ball my hands into fists.

"What exactly is your plan? To fall your way to the bottom? To carry your board and walk all the way down?" He swivels his board as he slides in front of me with ease. "We don't have the time."

"I already told you—"

He shakes his head. "Enough with the lies, Aspen. I'm not an idiot."

"That's debatable."

"Admit it. You're out of your league."

With a growl, I reach down and strap my loose boot onto the board and tighten the bindings. That much I know how to do. What comes next is my damn pride getting the better of me again.

I shimmy my legs forward until I'm away from the safety of the flat top of the hill and then slowly straighten my board so it's pointing downhill.

Baylor's laugh fades behind me as I bend my knees and center my weight and begin sliding down the steep hill. As I swiftly increase in speed, a silent alarm goes off in my head, telling me to slow down, to stop.

But I don't know how.

My pride dissipates as fear takes over, and my heart sinks from the unwanted rush of adrenaline. My arms swing as my balance wavers from my heels to my toes.

Other riders shout at me as I narrowly miss them.

The edge of my board digs into the snow, and before I can prepare myself, I fall face-first into the hill. The fresh powder Henry and his friends made out to be so wonderful does little to soften my blow, but I imagine falling on anything at the speed I was going is bound to hurt.

"Aspen!" I hear the person shouting my name getting closer.

I wipe the cold, partially melted snow from my face and roll my eyes.

"Are you insane?" Baylor asks, spraying up snow as he stops beside me.

I push myself up onto my hands and knees. "Why? Because I fantasize about castrating you over my morning coffee?"

There is a moment of silence before he lets out a low chuckle. "The first thing you think about in the morning is my cock, huh?"

"Ugh! Why don't you just leave me alone?" I throw myself upright and immediately topple over into Baylor's chest.

His arms wrap around my middle out of instinct, and we both go down together.

"Oof," I say, landing on my solid pillow.

Baylor grunts. "Wow. Graceful."

"You were in my way!"

"Your way of what exactly? Getting another face full of snow? By all means, go ahead."

I narrow my eyes at him and smack him in the chest. I try to wiggle myself off of him, but his arms around me tighten. "What are you doing?"

"When are you just going to admit I'm right?"

"In your dreams."

His goggles lift from the wicked grin that raises his cheeks. "You do a lot more than that in my dreams."

My mouth drops open, and I smack him again. "Ew!"

His stomach flexes under me with a laugh.

I fight his grasp on me, but he doesn't budge. "Let go, Baylor."

"Not a chance. Not until you admit you've never boarded in your life."

"I already told you that I have! Why are you obsessing over this?"

"Because when you come out here without any experience and start on this kind of hill, you're not only putting yourself in danger, but you're also putting others in danger!" His arms squeeze me tighter to make sure I'm paying attention.

I can't see his eyes, so all I can do is watch his lips as he scolds me.

"I didn't realize."

"Yeah, because all you were thinking about was yourself. Like always."

He finally releases his hold, and I sit back on my knees. "I *have* boarded. Once."

"Once?" Baylor pushes up onto his elbows. "That doesn't count as experience! Are you crazy?"

"You don't think I know that? That I don't regret coming up here? I'm under no impression that I'm going to get down this mountain safely. I'm terrified, okay? Are you happy?"

"Not exactly," he grumbles.

I dart my eyes to him, surprised to find that he's not gloating at all. "You're not?"

He pushes his goggles up so they're resting on his forehead. His piercing green eyes are even more vivid, surrounded by the bright white snow. "Well, I didn't want you up here from the beginning. But a part of me was kind of hoping you'd prove me wrong. I would've loved to eat my words actually. To see you tear it up out here. Why did you lie to everybody?"

"Isn't it obvious?"

His eyebrows rise as he waits for an explanation.

"You! You're always—ugh! You're always ruining everything!"

"You're kidding, right?"

I cross my arms as I sit back on my heels.

"Who's the one stuck on the side of the mountain right now, making it everyone's problem?"

"I wouldn't have had to lie if you didn't make things so difficult for me all the time."

His eyes narrow a fraction, but he doesn't say anything.

"Why are you so horrible to me?"

"Please." He laughs once. "Don't think you're so special. I'm horrible to everyone."

"You're not that horrible to Jesse, Luke, or Henry."

"They don't count."

"There's not one person in this world you care about other than yourself?"

Baylor looks down at his hands for a moment in thought and then quickly returns his attention to me with an even colder stare than before. If there is someone he does in fact care about, he isn't going to share it with me.

"So, you don't know how to carve?"

I sigh, shaking my head.

"How to stop?"

I shake my head again.

He nods because he already saw my graceful display and then stands up in front of me like it's nothing. His hands grip my elbows, and I balance on his forearms as I get my board underneath me again.

"What are you doing?" I ask, sounding more ungrateful than I should.

He frowns. "Helping you."

"Toward the nearest cliff?"

His lips tighten in a line as he suppresses a smile. "I mean, that's one way off the mountain, isn't it?"

I jerk my arms away from him.

He throws his head back and laughs. The sound he makes causes my stomach to flutter. "I'm joking! Come here."

"Why? You got your *I told you so* moment. Why aren't you leaving me in your dust?"

"It's either this or I have to explain to Henry how I left you up here. I don't think that scenario would be good for either one of us, would it?"

He's right. Henry would scold us both—Baylor for leaving me up here, me for putting myself in the situation. I'd get the worst of it because Henry wouldn't have expected this from me. The only time I have ever lied to Henry was when I told him I'd never played poker, but that was also how we met, so he ended up seeing that as a positive memory, not a negative one. It's an even better memory for me because I beat him.

If I don't get down this hill soon, Henry will probably come back up here to get me, if he isn't already on his way. I have no idea how long it takes to get down a freaking mountain. In my case, I might just have to accept the fact that this is my new home. I live here now. At least the view is nice.

Baylor smacks me once on the helmet. "Do you want to get off this mountain or not?"

I stare at him for a moment, anticipating him to burst out laughing because I fell for another one of his games but it never comes.

"So what you want to do is keep your weight centered. You ride goofy, so when—"

"Hey!" I frown.

"It's not a bad thing, Aspen. You either ride regular or goofy. It just depends on what end of the board you lead with."

"Oh." I'd blush if my cheeks weren't already red from the cold.

"I'm going to slide with you, and when I lean, I want you to lean with me."

"I'll try," I tell him, tightening my hands around his arms. If it hurts him, he doesn't show it.

He only smiles a fraction before looking out ahead of us at our path. I follow his gaze as we start to slide.

"Now, gently shift your weight from your heels to the balls of your feet. Dig that board into the mountain when I say, okay?" Baylor holds me firmly, giving me directions and explaining how the movements help us.

I nearly catch an edge again when I lean my weight back too far, but he pulls me forward just enough that I can regain my balance before we both topple over.

"Not bad. Keep your knees bent."

"I am!" I argue.

He shakes his head at me. "You're fucking stubborn, you know that?"

Something in his teasing tone makes me look up at him. There's a softness to his grin I haven't seen before.

He's still looking ahead, so it gives me a chance to see him up close without his intimidating eyes locked on me. But that one look, that split second, costs us.

My weight is too far back, and as I try to pull myself back upright, I end up pulling Baylor down on top of me instead. In an attempt to catch myself, my hand takes the brunt of the fall and gets pinned beneath me.

I scream out as soon as the stabbing pain ensues. "Ow! Fuck. Fuck. Fuck. Fuck. FUU—"

Baylor's eyes are wide as he scrambles off of me. "What's the matter? What happened?"

I cradle my injured wrist, forcing back tears. "Oh, just karma. Fucking karma."

# 4

# ASPEN IN ASPEN

I part my knees on the edge of the bench just outside the chalet to make room for the medic to inspect me closer. I can't help the smile that stretches across my face as I stare up at the twenty-something-year-old blond wrapping my wrist in an elastic bandage. His eyes are the color of the ocean, and his jawline is so sharp that it makes me want to bite it.

"It's just a sprain. Make sure you rest it for the first forty-eight hours, okay? Ice will help reduce the swelling." An adorable crease forms between his brows as he concentrates.

"I'm Aspen, by the way," I say, trying not to seem too obvious, but just obvious enough.

"Shaun." The smile I get in return tells me I'm not the only one interested. "Aspen in Aspen, huh? You should check out the gift shop. Your name is everywhere."

I giggle at his lame joke at the same time I hear Baylor's not-so-subtle groan from the other side of the table.

"Jesus, fuck," Baylor mutters.

"Ignore him," I tell Shaun and purse my lips.

Baylor clicks his tongue and points over at the bandage on my wrist. "Is that really necessary?"

Shaun finishes wrapping the bandage. "Compression helps, yes."

"What about drinks? Would that help too?" I bite my lower lip.

Shaun gives Baylor a wary glance.

He returns my gaze, looking hesitant. "Uh, I wouldn't recommend drinking with any painkillers you plan on taking, but a beer or two might take the edge off."

"Try *cranberry vodka*," Baylor mumbles just loud enough that I hear him.

My brows twitch in surprise. He's been around me drinking plenty of times to know I hate beer, but I'm still shocked that he's paid enough attention to me to remember my favorite drink.

"There's a good bar off the main road here that some of my friends frequent. The Tipsy Tavern," Shaun suggests as he zips up his backpack full of medical supplies.

Baylor rises, looking down at his phone. "We prefer the bar Heights."

I roll my eyes as I tuck my injured wrist carefully beneath my sleeve. "I'm sure the guys wouldn't mind trying out a new place."

"Guys?" Shaun asks.

"You know they would." Baylor finishes a text and saunters around the table, grabbing both of our boards from the holding rack. "Henry's asking where we are. Let's go."

I'm not sure if Shaun has been picking up on my subtle invite or my flirting for that matter, but I don't want to wait around all day, wondering if he has. "Do you want to join me—er, us for a drink later?"

Shaun laughs. "Do you come as a package deal?"

"Well, no. But I'm here with my friends …"

Baylor shifts his weight impatiently next to me. Whatever look he's giving Shaun must not be a good one based on the way his face pinches into a frown and he stands a little taller.

"I could meet you somewhere within walking distance of Heights instead?" I offer.

"No, no. I don't want you walking around in the freezing cold just so I can see you again." Shaun gives me a warm smile and shakes his head. "I'd love to have a drink with you. What time should I be there?"

My stomach flutters as I grin. I swat my good hand at Baylor's chest, unable to tear my focus away from Shaun.

Baylor flinches when I make contact. "Ow."

"What time should he meet me, Baylor?" I urge.

There's a long silence. I don't know if he's not sure about the time we are planning on being there or if he doesn't want to answer, but I presume the latter. I'm about to swat his chest again when he finally answers.

"Six thirty." He releases the words through clenched teeth.

"Perfect. I'm off at six," Shaun says, making more eye contact with Baylor than he does me.

My phone buzzes in my pocket for the third time since I got down the mountain on the back of Shaun's snowmobile. I know every one of them has been from Henry, but I haven't had a chance to answer until now.

"Okay, great! I'll see you later tonight, Shaun. I gotta take this, sorry. Thanks again!" I say, holding my wrist up before answering my phone. "Hello?"

"You are alive," Henry replies with a hint of annoyance. "I thought Baylor might've led you off a cliff or something."

"Maybe I led him off one," I counter.

His laugh is bright. "I considered that, but *he* texted me back. What happened to you? You said you would be right behind me, and then you disappeared."

"I'm sorry. I ran into a bit of a … hiccup." I scan the tan bandage around my throbbing wrist. "I thought Baylor filled you in?"

He pauses. "He just told me he ran into you at the chalet. Did something happen? Are you okay?"

I peer over at Baylor curiously. He's finishing some sort of weird handshake with Shaun—a much different interaction than they were having a moment ago. I narrow my eyes at him when he meets my stare.

"Oh. Yeah. Like I said, Henry, it was just a hiccup. I'm okay."

"If you're hurt and he had anything to do with it …"

*And cue protective-brother mode.*

"I said I'm fine! But I think I'm going to just hang out in the chalet the rest of the day. Drink some hot cocoa. Read a book on my phone. Maybe call my parents and catch up."

"So, you are hurt." There's anger in his voice.

"It's just a sprain. Nothing is broken."

"A sprain? Aspen! How the hell did you do that?"

"I … fell on it."

My thoughts wander back to the moment I tried to catch myself, and I realize that I could've walked away with a much worse injury if Baylor hadn't offered to help me. Something about that puzzles me, but there are some things about Baylor Frost that will always remain a mystery to me.

"I've seen your clumsy ass trip and fall on hard ground all the time. How the hell did you manage to fall in the snow and sprain your—what is it that you sprained?"

"My wrist. Again, totally fine. In fact, it kind of worked out. This hot medic took care of me. I invited him out for drinks with us tonight."

"Whoa, his job title is *ski patrol*." Baylor appears beside me. "Don't make it sound sexy."

"Is that Baylor? Let me talk to him," Henry demands.

"You already talked to him."

"That was before I had all the information, and I have a feeling you're still not telling me everything," Henry says. His instincts are too good. Law school has him scrutinizing everything lately. "Hand him the phone."

"Don't tell me what to do."

"Damn it, Aspen. Stop being difficult."

"And now, you're asking me to change everything about myself. Rude," I say with mock exasperation. I'm glad he can't see my face.

"What's that smile for, Pen?"

I look around and immediately spot Henry trudging toward us in his skis. I giggle to myself as I hang up.

"What am I going to do with you?" Henry's face falls when he lifts my wrist with a delicate hand. "You know anything about this?" He nods at Baylor.

Baylor's jaw clenches before he speaks. "You seriously think I'd intentionally hurt her?"

"I don't know. Would you?"

I roll my eyes and pull my hand out of Henry's grasp. "Ugh, let it go already. I fell. I got hurt. I need some ice. Preferably in a glass with some liquor. Okay?"

The side of Henry's mouth pulls up as he steps out of his skis. "How about a hot chocolate and a couple of aspirin?" He wraps an arm around my shoulders and leads me inside the chalet.

"Where are Jesse and Luke?" Baylor asks.

Henry tilts his head and raises a brow, answering him without a word. Baylor and I don't need any further explanation. They found girls.

Baylor tosses his helmet on the table and laughs. "They don't waste a second, do they?"

Sounds like I won't be the only one with a date tonight.

After stripping out of my snow gear, I'm left with my university sweatshirt, yoga pants, and boots for my date at Heights. Not to mention, my curls have all been matted down from my helmet. Every time I try to smooth it out, my fingers get stuck in knots. It's not the effort I usually put into first dates, but I didn't exactly plan on meeting a hot medic and asking him out.

Though I've never gone on a date with four other men there, too, so I'm not sure if you can even count this as an official date.

"Hey. You okay?" Jesse asks, giving me a hand as I jump out of the truck.

"Yeah. Why?" I smile.

"You look nervous."

Baylor slams his door shut and twists his baseball cap around backward. "Of course she's nervous. She's got a hot date," he teases.

"Jealous?"

Baylor scoffs. "I'll be surprised if he even shows."

I raise my chin and smirk. "Aw, you are jealous."

"Don't worry, Baylor. I like to share." Luke flashes Baylor a devilish grin.

Jesse pats him on the back as we head through the double-door entrance. "Yeah, man. Take your pick. I'm not greedy."

Henry laughs at the way my face scrunches in disgust.

"I can't believe you associate with these guys."

"We're all cut from the same cloth, I suppose." He ruffles the top of my hair.

I quickly pat it back down and glare at him. "Yeah? Then, how come you're not meeting some girl here and passing her around to all your friends?"

He leans on the bar on his elbows and gestures to the bartender at the other end. "Because I'm here with you."

I roll my eyes. He knows that doesn't count.

"And besides," he adds, "I prefer a bit more exclusivity with the women I share a bed with."

Come to think of it, I've never seen Henry take anyone home after a night we spent out together. I've stopped by his apartment a handful of times before class and gotten to meet his late-night endeavors before they left, but that's it. Henry is very private about that part of his life. Not just with his guy friends, but with me too.

The bartender appears before I can dwell on that thought.

"What can I get you both?"

"Hey there. Can I get a bottle of Pappy and some glasses to that table in the corner, please?" He points to the green velvet booth, where Baylor, Jesse, and Luke are sitting down.

The man's brows rise a fraction at Henry's request. Henry has always been a guy with expensive taste, especially his liquor, so I'm not surprised at the bartender's reaction to a college student ordering what I imagine to be a very pricey bottle.

Henry slides him a card from his wallet.

"Right away, sir."

Henry nods at the man with appreciation and then tilts his head down at me. "What would you like, Aspen? I know you hate bourbon."

"Uh, cranberry vodka, I guess." I shrug.

"Do you have a preference of vodka, miss?" the bartender asks.

I stare blankly at the glass bottles behind the bar. Some of the fancy ones without labels make me question if the bartender mixes drinks or science experiments.

"Goose is fine, right, Pen?" Henry answers for me.

"Sure." I offer him a smile while the man in the white button-up and plaid vest gets started on our order.

"So, tell me more about this guy you met today," Henry says, leading me to the table.

"I didn't get a chance to really get to know him before he had to go back to work. But he seems sweet."

"Sweet, huh?" A small dimple appears on his cheek. "You always go for the nice guys."

"Would you rather I go out with the bad guys then?" I smirk.

"Not at all. You just seem to get bored of the nice ones. I think it'd be good for you to find someone who challenges you. And not so—"

"Boring?" I laugh.

He has a point. I don't have a great track record with holding on to the few guys I've dated in college. In my defense, the only men I surround myself with when I go out are Henry and his friends, and that doesn't exactly elicit a lot of courageous men willing to ask if I belong to one of them or not. I think most guys just assume I'm taken or they don't want to date someone who is only friends with guys.

"Am I going to like him?"

"You like everybody. Them"—I point to our table, full of his friends—"no."

All three heads sitting in the booth swivel to look at me.

"What's that now?" Luke asks, resting an arm on the back of the booth.

"Aspen here was just telling me how much you're not going to like her date because you all are a bunch of judgmental cunts."

"Whoa!" Baylor feigns insult.

Luke raises his hand to his chest. "Harsh!"

"I did not say that!"

Henry smirks and slides into the booth after me.

"Yet," I add, scooting in next to Jesse.

"What did we ever do to you, Aspen?" Jesse pouts.

I click my tongue when I look at him.

"Oh, here we go." Henry chuckles.

"On my twenty-first birthday, you spilled your drink on my dress, and instead of apologizing, you told me its value went up because the drink cost more than what I'd paid for it."

Jesse winces. "That wasn't my finest hour, but to be fair, I wasn't wrong."

I move my attention to Baylor and shake my head. "Ugh, I'd need a decade to even skim the surface with you."

My eyes move on to Luke, but he raises his hands in surrender before I can start on him.

"Oh no. I've made peace with who I am, and I don't apologize for it."

"That's right," Baylor chimes in, fingering the black cord and silver chain necklaces beneath his half-zip. "There's nothing wrong with having standards."

"Standards?" I ask mockingly, snapping my eyes away from his chest.

Baylor nods, further egging me on.

"Pff. Standards are good for the self-respecting individual, but yours are so far up your ass that it's amazing anyone can measure up."

Henry throws his head back, releasing that familiar, warm laugh I love.

"Yeah, well, it's amazing you have any at all." Baylor suppresses a smile as he holds my gaze.

Our drinks get delivered, and his eyes drop to the cranberry liquor being pushed in front of me. The perfectly square ice cubes clank against the crystal glass, and a spear of frosted cranberries and rosemary balances on the rim for garnish.

*Rosemary? What the—*

"What's with the rosemary?" Baylor reiterates my thoughts. His eyes are still on my drink, and a smile tugs at the corner of his mouth.

*Ugh.* I hate the look of smug satisfaction that he gets when he's right about something. So he knows my favorite drink. Big whoop. I'm a rather predictable person. I haven't had much else to drink since I spent the night hovering over a toilet my freshman year of college, after a dizzy night out with some friends and one too many mixed cocktails. I prefer to stick with drinks that I know won't make me sick, and that brings me comfort. And right now, my tart cranberry bliss in a cup is all the comfort I need to ease my nerves before Shaun arrives.

I glance at the doors as a middle-aged couple walks through, and my shoulders slump. It's only five minutes past the hour. Shaun could be looking for parking.

I try to distract myself and tune in to whatever Luke is going on about, but I can't help but look at the doors every time they open.

My fingers pull at the elastic hem of my sweatshirt an hour and two drinks later. "Maybe I should've gone to The Tipsy Tavern instead."

Henry swallows back some liquor before fixing me with a quizzical stare. "What?"

"It's the bar Shaun mentioned. I probably wouldn't have stood out so much there. Look at me. Look at this place." I laugh.

"You would've stood out there too," Baylor says, meeting my eyes from across the table.

My brows draw together. "What's that supposed to mean?"

He flashes a devilish grin that oozes mockery and makes my cheeks ignite.

I pinch the end of the sugared toothpick on my drink and fling it across the table before Baylor sees it coming.

He jumps back as it hits him just below his throat. "What the hell?"

A giggle bursts from my lips when I see the rosemary fall beneath the collar of his shirt.

He quickly stands, trying to shake the rosemary loose. As soon as it escapes and drops to the floor, his gaze snaps to mine.

The menacing grin on my face falls when I see the red drops of cranberry juice left behind on the collar of his shirt.

Baylor notices and yanks his shirt out to see for himself, baring teeth when he finds the stain. "What the fuck is your problem? Why would you do that?"

"Aye, calm down. I'm sure she meant no harm." Henry waves his hand at him.

Jesse and Luke snicker to themselves.

Baylor clenches his fists at his sides. I can almost see the steam starting to spew from his ears. It's funny how upset he's getting. But the anger on his face swiftly turns into a menacing smile.

I bite my lip warily.

"What's that look for?" Jesse nods at Baylor, but his eyes are still homed in on me.

"You know, I was beginning to feel a shred of guilt for paying your ski-patrol boy toy not to come tonight, but now, I don't really give a fuck. I hope he doesn't show."

"Wait …" I peer around the table to see if everyone heard the same thing as me. "What?"

Luke folds his hands behind his head and leans back. "Shit, man. You pulled that card?"

Jesse blows out air through his lips in disbelief.

My stomach tightens. "Did you just say you paid him off?"

Henry thrusts his hand through his hair. "Ah, man. You didn't seriously play that bullshit on her, did you?"

Baylor nods slowly. "The guy took it like he'd won the fucking lottery."

A ringing in my ears fills the brief silence. Heat rises up my back, over my shoulders, and onto my cheeks. My hand circles my glass in a choke hold as I try to process and come up with a response. I have the urge to throw the whole glass in his face, to stain the rest of his shirt bright red.

Instead, I mutter the question I can't seem to find the answer to. "Why?"

Baylor huffs. "Because I knew he'd take it."

"That doesn't answer my question." I shake my head.

"To make out his character." Jesse sighs.

Luke nods as he twirls his newly empty glass on the oak table.

Henry tosses back a finger or two of whiskey and glares at his friend. "You didn't have to. She's perfectly capable of finding a decent guy."

"Wait a second. Is this something you all do? Humiliate others for sport and then tell them it was for their own good?" I stand.

"Pen, come on." Henry pinches the bridge of his nose. "It's not like that at all."

"I guess I shouldn't be surprised. You guys tend to humiliate plenty of people just by being your own arrogant, entitled selves. Am I your entertainment for the night. Is that it?"

"Well, Baylor might be enjoying this more than he should, but we do this to weed out the bad ones," Henry explains.

"You're backing up his actions? Seriously?" I laugh.

"Try and look at it as a sign of respect. We've done it for Henry's sister a few times. It works like a charm." Jesse's smile falls when I narrow my eyes at him.

"Yeah. One guy actually threw the money back in my face." Luke chuckles.

Henry tips his glass at him. "I actually liked that guy."

Jesse's smile reappears. "Didn't Clara end up hating him?"

I fold my arms, not finding humor in any of this. "You're unbelievable, all of you."

Henry pulls at my elbow to try and get me to sit back down, but I swat him away. "Think about it, Pen. Do you really want to be with a guy who is willing to accept a couple hundred dollars to stand you up? If he was really into you, no amount of money would have been enough."

"Besides, it's not like we threaten them." Luke shrugs. "They get the cash up front. A smart man would take the money *and* the date."

"You've all made more money just by being born than he's made in his entire life, working! He wasn't handed a life of privilege and fortune. He has a day job, making less in a week than you carry around in your pockets. Of course he's going to take the money! That doesn't make him a bad person." My gaze meets Baylor's. "It just means he knows the value of a penny more than you ever will."

# 5

# COZY

As if a sprained wrist isn't enough, last night's debacle gives me another excuse to sleep in the next morning while the boys leave for day two on the slopes.

I didn't have a desire to stay at the bar after Baylor's humiliating stunt. Henry understood and drove us all home, which meant Jesse's and Luke's dates were ruined as well. They were a little prickly about it on the car ride back to the cabin, so I doubt they want to spend another day with the possibility of me cockblocking them again. I think it's best we all have a little time to cool off anyway. And all I can hope is that Baylor cools off with his head deep in a snowbank somewhere far away from me.

"How much snow has to be covering you to suffocate?" I ask Henry's chef before sipping my coffee.

Marta pauses mid-whisk when she notices I am speaking to her. Her brow moves up her forehead, and she shakes her head in a way that tells me she doesn't understand my question. Her English is somewhat poor, but she understands enough to argue her way into making me breakfast.

When I was growing up, my dad spent most nights at the casino, and my mom worked late, so I had to learn to cook for myself. I'm no chef, but the self-taught lessons have served me well in college on a budget. I can turn a fifty-cent ramen packet into a mean gourmet meal. But I can tell Marta doesn't feel comfortable with someone else doing her job, so I didn't put up much of a fight. I did, however, bargain to make dinner for the house one night while I'm here. I still have yet to decide what I'm going to cook, but that gives me time to find out if Baylor has any allergies.

Marta continues whisking the eggs for my omelet when I hear footsteps rounding the corner.

Baylor shuffles into the kitchen in boxer briefs.

*Only* boxer briefs.

"What the hell are you still doing here?" I set my mug down on the countertop harder than intended.

Baylor glances over at me indifferently but doesn't respond.

Marta greets him with a bright smile that showcases the creases by her eyes and the dimples on her cheeks and says something to him in her native language.

To my surprise, Baylor responds effortlessly while gesturing to different ingredients she has set up beside the stove. Once Marta begins cracking more eggs into a bowl,

Baylor pours himself a cup of coffee and grabs an orange from the fruit bowl in the center of the island.

I shift in my seat, uncomfortable with how much I like hearing those words fall from his lips. "How do you know how to speak …" I pause, unsure of what language that even was.

"My mother is Polish." The two emerald eyes that peer up at me from the rim of his mug make my insides flutter. "Czech and Polish are very similar languages." He shrugs and finishes another sip.

"I didn't know your mother was Polish."

He holds my eyes in thought. "Is there much you do know about me?"

It never occurred to me how easy it was for me to picture Baylor's family a certain way. His father is the head of the underworld—because, naturally, Baylor is the spawn of Satan. He has a fiery torch and everything. And I guess I always thought his mother was absent, like Jesse's are, because I've only ever heard him reference his dad in conversation.

I think I just put him into a certain category based on the few things I do know about him and the way he's treated me. The fact that he is getting me to doubt my judgment on him with one simple question irritates me. I don't need to know anything about his personal life to rationalize why I don't like him. It certainly wouldn't excuse his actions toward me over the last couple of years.

The thoughts spiral in my head, and I shake them away.

"Why didn't you leave with everyone earlier?" I demand rather than ask.

There's a hint of amusement on his face that he tries to hide by biting his lower lip. "I overslept."

"And they didn't wake you?"

"No." He laughs. "Henry might be a softy for you, but he's not the most patient or considerate. Besides, it was nice to get some beauty sleep in."

He stretches, and my eyes wander down his trimmed torso without thought. He catches me lingering on a rather mouthwatering area below his waistline, and he clears his throat, fixing me with a heated stare.

"You're going to have to stop fucking me with your eyes, Penny, or I'm going to think you want something from me."

My mouth snaps shut at the same time my eyes bulge in Marta's direction. I start to shake my head. "I wasn't—"

"Relax. *Eye-fucking* isn't in her vocabulary. At least, I don't think it is." He scrunches his nose in a teasing way.

Marta turns and sets my hot plate down with an expression that says she's none the wiser, and my shoulders relax.

"You're so … annoying."

"That's the best you've got today?"

"It's too early. Can I eat my breakfast in peace, please?"

"Suit yourself."

Marta hands him his omelet, and he grins widely, showing off his gleaming white smile.

"I still think a good lay would do you some good. I'll be around. Let me know if your appetite changes," he adds with a smug little wink before disappearing from the kitchen.

When I look back down at my cheesy mushroom and onion omelet, I'm suddenly famished, and I devour it in no time. After breakfast, I take a quick shower, style my hair with some waves, and put on a slouchy sweater dress my mom gifted me. It feels like a giant blanket and is perfect for curling up on the couch in Henry's theater room.

Marta is kind enough to let me pop my own popcorn when I pass through the kitchen to grab snacks. To no surprise, Henry has a large inventory of his favorite popcorn, which, coincidentally, is my favorite too. I make two bags in case he comes back from skiing early and wants to join me.

By the time the opening credits begin on my first Hallmark movie, I'm settled into the center cushion of the most comfortable couch I've ever sat on.

"This could be dangerous," I tell myself as I wiggle deeper into the pillows and shovel popcorn into my mouth.

"What is?"

A chill runs up my spine at the sound of his voice. Maybe if I don't say anything and I keep real still, he'll go away.

The couch dips beside me, and I have to stretch my neck to see over the pillow. Welp. So much for that theory.

"What are we watching?" Baylor chirps.

I shake my head. This isn't happening. "Nope."

He reaches for my popcorn and manages to grab a handful before I can pull it away. "What do you mean?"

"Nope. Nope. Nope. Not happening. I call dibs on this room today. You can have the rest of the house, okay? Please. Just leave me and my movies alone."

"No can do."

"Look, you're way ahead of whatever score you're keeping in your head after last night. All I'm asking for is a moment of peace."

The seconds tick by without a smart retort from him. So long that I have to remove the pillow between us to make sure he didn't fall asleep on me. It would've been awfully fast, but I'm convinced this couch has superpowers.

Baylor cranes his head to look at me. He's sitting closer than I thought.

"What are you doing?" I narrow my eyes at him.

The side of his mouth pulls up as he holds his pointer finger up to his lips in a hush motion. "I'm giving you your moment."

I let out a long sigh in defeat. "I don't have the energy to fight you today, Baylor."

Trying to unwedge myself from the cozy crevasse I formed with one arm is more difficult than I expected. Even more so when a warm arm circles my waist and pulls me back.

"Let me make a deal with you." His breath hits my ear, and I shiver.

"Only if the deal is you removing your arm before I bite it off." I put as much threat in my voice as possible.

His large frame shakes silently with mirth as he leans into my side. "You watch one movie of my choice, and I'll leave you alone for the rest of the day."

I look up at the screen, grinding my teeth together.

He points up at the redhead pulling a suitcase down a snow-covered road in heeled boots and a thin designer jacket. "I can already tell you how this plays out. That rich city girl falls for the farm boy in the middle of bumfuck nowhere and pays off his family's debt, so they can keep the farm. He realizes she's not what he expected and tells her he loves her. She ends up staying. The end."

I cover my mouth to hide my smile, but he sees and pulls my hand away.

"I'm right, aren't I?" He stares down at my lips.

I bite my lip and giggle. "Way to ruin it."

His eyes soften as he watches me for a beat, and then he loosens his arm around my waist. My stomach twists with embarrassment at how quickly I miss the warmth.

"Do we have a deal?" he asks.

I purse my lips as I consider it. How bad can it be anyway? If it truly is a Christmas movie, the chances of me liking it are drastically high. As long as it isn't *Die Hard*. My dad and I argue every year about whether that movie is a holiday movie or not. At the time, it's infuriating, but now, it kind of makes me smile.

"Can I take that smile as a yes?"

"Fine," I reluctantly agree.

Baylor hops off the couch to fetch the remote. Before he returns, he reaches into a drawer in front of the television and pulls out a handful of different kinds of candy. I perk my head upright as he kicks the drawer shut with his foot, but I'm too stubborn to ask him to get me something.

I'm still eyeing the candy drawer when Baylor settles back into the couch beside me and hits play on his movie. He tosses a box of Red Vines into my lap, and I practically squeal with excitement.

I'm tearing the package open as I turn and look at him. "How did you—"

"Shh." He nods at the screen. "It's starting."

To know my favorite drink is one thing, but to know my favorite candy is … ugh, it's confusing. He shouldn't know anything about me. He's too observant. What possible motive can he have for that? Or for sitting here with me when he could be doing anything else? He could watch whatever this black-

and-white movie is upstairs in the family room. Granted, that TV is much smaller than this one, but it's not like you can call any of the televisions in this place small. He could play pool in the study or take out one of the snowmobiles I saw in the garage. Hell, he could be outside, carving an ice sculpture of himself for all I care. But instead, he's chosen to sit here with me.

I study his sharp features as the movie lights up his face, hoping to discover any ill intentions. The muscles of his jaw flex under recently shaven skin as he works the candy in his mouth. The skin is smooth and the muscles taut—my favorite combination. I've seen the same muscles dance when he's crossed with me about something, when I'm being stubborn, or sometimes, when he's trying to suppress laughter. Baylor eating candy while watching his favorite Christmas movie is a new one, and I take a mental note of it.

His tongue swipes across his lower lip, wetting it, and I can't help but lick my own in response.

"What are you thinking about, Penny?" he rasps.

His eyes are hidden beneath lowered lashes, but I know he's watching me. I can feel his piercing stare, even in the dark. He's been watching me long enough to know that I was watching him.

I swallow the dry lump in my throat and run my fingers through my hair, forcing my attention back to the screen.

"You fight your attraction to me so poorly." Baylor's deep voice makes my insides buzz.

I don't look at him. "I'm not fighting anything."

The movie fills the silence that falls between us, but I can feel his smile burning into the side of my face.

A beat passes. And then another. And another.

I scooch down in my seat, hoping some of the couch can block his view of me, but my not-so-graceful movement makes my dress scrunch up at my waist, exposing my entire thigh and hip crease. The heat I feel on my face from his stare travels down my side and settles on my bare hip. I should cover myself, but I freeze instead because my fight-or-flight instincts are apparently broken. That, and my ability to think straight.

The couch dips as he leans in next to my ear, and I stiffen. "Do you still think about your first night here? I do. I know it was only days ago, but it feels longer." His knuckles dance along my thigh with the lightest touch. "You were so wet, weren't you?"

My cheeks warm at his starkness. "I'd just gotten out of the shower."

He breathes out a laugh that tickles my neck. "You know that's not what I mean. You can't tell me that if I had slid my fingers between your legs, you wouldn't have been ready for me." His hand stretches over my leg and flexes.

I feel the same pressure from that night building and press my thighs together.

"You're ready for me right now, aren't you?" He pulls my dress over my shoulder and brushes his lips against my skin. "This dress looks more like it was meant to fall off of you than it was to be worn by you." His mouth moves inward across my collarbone.

I shudder and let my head fall a little to the side. "Baylor, don't."

"Why? Do you actually want me to stop? Or do you just hate the fact that you want this more than you're willing to admit?"

He pulls back slowly, kisses my shoulder again, and then tastes me. The heat of his tongue sends shivers over my skin.

My eyes close as I stifle a groan. "I want you to stop because I know you're messing with me, like you always do."

He's never used these types of measures to get under my skin, but I can only presume he's testing out new tactics.

I take a steady breath, trying to calm my pounding heart, and then turn to level him with a look of warning. "I'm not falling for it, okay? This is just another game to you."

I can feel his breath against the corner of my mouth right before the enticing scent of sweet cinnamon hits my nose. My mouth waters.

He hesitates mere centimeters from my lips with a strangely vulnerable look in his eyes. "What if it's not?"

There's a softness to Baylor's voice he shouldn't possess. I'm used to the one that boasts confidence and breathes threats. This voice turns me to mush and makes my head foggy. I resent it. At least, I would if I could just stop staring at his lips. God, they're perfect. I wonder how many girls have gotten to kiss them, to feel the hot touch of them claim the soft peaks of their breasts.

My tongue wets my lips at the thought.

"Aspen, you down here?" Henry calls from a distance, sending off a silent alarm in my brain.

"Shh." Baylor grins and tries to hide us both by lying on top of me, but he's left to catch himself as I scurry out from underneath him and flee from the movie room.

I turn the corner of the staircase when Henry almost plows me over.

"Whoa!" Henry catches me with his hands on my shoulders.

"You're back early." I rush the words out. I'm flushed all over, and I hope he doesn't notice.

"Yeah, the winds were unbearable, so we decided to call it quits." Faint windburn colors the tops of his cheeks. "Did I interrupt something?"

My heart skips. "What do you mean?"

He nods down at my hands. Somehow, in the midst of my escape, I managed to hold on to my popcorn bowl.

"Oh! I was trying to watch a movie, but then Baylor decided to join me, and, well—" I teeter my head, hoping he can fill in the blanks on his own. The last thing he'd think Baylor would do is try to kiss me.

*Baylor tried to kiss me. Me!*

Sounds from the movie echo down the hallway, and Henry's face lights up with recognition. "Ah, you're watching *It's a Wonderful Life*? I love this one!" He yanks the bowl out of my hands, and shoves a handful of popcorn in his face. "Come on. I'll be your defense, Pen."

I turn slowly on my heels and follow him back into the dark theater room.

Baylor is still in the same spot, upright.

I'm relieved when Henry takes the seat next to him and gives him some sort of bro handshake.

"What's up, man? I thought you weren't feeling well?"

Baylor glances over Henry's shoulder at me and then back at Henry. "Guess I just needed some rest. How was it out there?"

A weird fluttering happens in my stomach when I realize he lied to his friends about staying back this morning. I can't help but feel that he did that to stay here with me.

"Eh, you didn't miss much. The weather wasn't great. I ran into those guys from the Kenrick Group my father does business with though."

Baylor smirks. "Shit. We need to play cards with them again soon. I need to win my money back. Those fuckers took me for fifty K!"

Henry jabs him with an elbow. "Way ahead of you. They'll be over on Christmas Eve."

Baylor swivels his head to me and then furrows a brow at Henry. "Really?"

"Yeah. Why not?"

Baylor nods in my direction, and Henry drops his shoulders.

"You know she can handle herself. I mean, she handles you just fine."

I smile.

"That's different." The worry grows on Baylor's face.

I raise a brow. Henry's dad doesn't exactly do business with the best of men. He likely invited them out of respect for his dad or, from the sounds of it, to get a little revenge on their wallets.

"It's just dinner and some poker. You know, in the spirit of Christmas." Henry finally looks at me. "You don't have to play if you don't want to. We'll be down here in the bar, so you can stay upstairs if it makes you uncomfortable."

"It's okay, Henry." I nod my head and smile at how considerate he is. "Like you said, I can handle myself. I probably won't play though."

I'm familiar with gambling. My dad's addiction to it was the root of all the arguments between my parents for most of my childhood and the main source of father-daughter bonding. When I started beating him and I was old enough to go to the casino, he'd beg me to come with him to help out the family. I won him nine hundred my first night there. Twelve hundred the next. And then nearly six thousand. I can understand how someone could grow addicted to something like that, especially after seeing my parents' faces light up when they saw how much I'd won. But that feeling quickly faded when my dad put it right back into the game and lost.

I don't want to be like him and be obsessed with money. Money gives people a false sense of power. And then when it's taken away from you, you're willing to do anything to get it back. Even if it means ruining the security and happiness of those around you.

I swore to myself I wouldn't play again unless it was just to have fun with friends and the stakes were pieces of gum and whatever else was in your pockets. But I found myself in a bind freshman year and needed a little extra cash to get by. Going to school on a partial scholarship is great and all, but I still have to come up with the other half of tuition, and Columbia isn't cheap. Not to mention, the cost of living in New York almost matches the price of a single textbook. My parents couldn't help me—not that I'd ever ask—and my part-time job at the campus coffee shop wasn't cutting it, so I had to come up with a solution. Cards were the fastest way I knew how to earn money.

And I'm forever grateful I went to that party with my tail between my legs because that was also the night I met Henry. After beating every cent out of him, he practically begged me to be friends with him.

"I don't think she could afford the buy-in anyway." Baylor's voice rips me out of my thoughts and ignites my skin.

"Oh, I got you, Pen." Henry winks.

The soft glow from the television lights up Baylor's face as it etches with disapproval. He opens his mouth to say something, but when I drag my bottom lip through my teeth, he snaps it back shut.

A smile tugs at my mouth when I realize I have an effect on him. I'm not sure what that means or why I enjoy it so much, but the fine line I drew between him and me a long time ago is beginning to fade. It scares me, but it also excites me in a curious way.

"Maybe I'll take you up on that, Henry," I say, giving Baylor a sly grin.

Baylor's jaw tics as he stares me down behind Henry's shoulders, and I'm instantly reminded of the dull ache between my thighs.

# 6

# MOUNTAIN AIR

It's been snowing for two days straight. The plows couldn't keep up, so the five of us have been keeping ourselves busy while we're snowed in.

I watched the boys play pool while sipping on one of Jesse's famous hot toddies. Their competitive banter can be entertaining, especially when Luke is losing.

Henry took me on a quick ride on one of his snowmobiles after breakfast yesterday morning. I hadn't ridden one since I was a kid.

We all watched a couple of hockey games together, and then I read a little while they soaked in the hot tub. Luke kept trying to get me to join them—my guess was, to get me in a bikini. But the snow was coming down too hard, and I didn't want to catch a cold.

I took the bandage off my wrist when I was on the phone with my mom this afternoon. It's still a little tender, but luckily, it wasn't my dominant hand I fell on.

It's been a fun couple of days, but even in a large cabin like this, I still can't help but feel like the walls are closing in. I notice Baylor more than I used to, not that he has ever been the unobtrusive type. His piercing green eyes aren't so cold anymore, and his presence doesn't make me want to jump out of the nearest window. But that could just be my mind playing tricks on me after the day in the theater room. I keep replaying it over and over in my head, like a dream I can't make sense of. Every lingering stare or subtle touch he's given me since is a reminder of it too.

All of it makes me dizzy. If Baylor wasn't trying to trick me, what's changed since we've been here to make him suddenly want me?

I stand in front of the bay window, watching the snow fall on the ground outside. My hands squeeze a mug of hot cocoa, savoring the warmth it brings. The smell of pine from the decorated tree beside me dances between the notes of rich chocolate, and I breathe in deep as I shut my eyes.

"You know what would make this better?"

My eyes flutter back open when Baylor's velvety whisper hits my ear. The heat from his chest covers my back, and I'm unable to stop myself from leaning back into him a little.

"Mistletoe."

My pulse picks up.

"Henry's gotta have one around here somewhere. Look at this place." He glances around at the vast decorations covering the cabin from top to bottom.

There's not a wooden post, railing, or mantel missing garland and twinkling lights. I think there's a decked-out tree in every room here too.

Although Henry's parents are halfway around the world, I know they still wanted to make sure this place felt like Christmas to him.

My friend's laughter echoes up from the basement. Henry wanted to play a few rounds of poker with the guys to get in some practice before tomorrow. I thought Baylor was with them, too, but clearly, I was wrong.

Baylor's hand skims my waist. "Should we go look for one together?"

"What?" I ask.

"A mistletoe. I thought I saw one above my showerhead now that I think about it."

I look over my shoulder and up at him. "Why are you doing this, Baylor?"

"Doing what?" He steps closer, angling his head toward mine.

"Trying to fuck me, like the last two years of hating each other never happened?" I place my hand on his chest as he begins to lean into my words. "What if I were to say yes? What if I took your hand and let you lead me up to your bedroom? Would you really lay me down and strip me bare? What would you do?" I originally wanted to see what his intentions were, to see if he'd really go through with it. Now, it's just fun, seeing him squirm. "Would you be sweet? Gentle? Or would you fuck me until I was on the brink of an orgasm, gasping for air, and then make me beg for it?"

His eyes pin me with a dark stare, filling me with anticipation.

Oh, he's definitely the kind of guy who likes to hear a girl beg.

There's a charge in the air. My nerves are on end. I can feel everything—from the way my hair floats along the side of my neck from the faint breeze of the ceiling fan to the fabric of my sweater rubbing my breasts over my mesh bra.

Something is going to happen.

Something is *finally* going to happen if I don't stop it.

And I don't want something to happen. *Right?*

I dart around him before I can give myself an honest answer. I set my mug down on the nearest flat surface and hurry toward the mudroom.

"Aspen?" Baylor calls from behind me.

I ignore him as I grab Clara's snow pants and jacket from the closet.

Baylor watches me with an equal measure of confusion and amusement as I hop into the pants and retrieve my snow boots from beneath the bench. As soon as I slip my feet inside them, I begin tying the strings into knots like there's an emergency.

I mean, there kind of is.

"What the hell are you doing?"

I thread my arms through the jacket and pull out the gloves I tucked in the pockets when I went snowboarding.

"Aspen, what is this? It's too cold out."

I don't answer him again.

"Hey!" His tone is deliciously demanding. "Where are you going?"

"I need some air," I tell him.

Shoving a hat and goggles over my head, I snatch a set of keys off a hook with a tag that reads *Polaris.*

Baylor's eyes widen before I throw the garage door open, and he follows after me. "You can't go out there alone! It'll be dark soon!"

I swing my leg over the neon-green sled, turn it over, and rev the engine.

"Seriously, Aspen, turn it off! Now!" he growls.

I make the engine sing again. "What? I can't hear you!" I cover my smile with the neck guard on my jacket.

Baylor reaches for my wrist, but I launch myself forward before he can touch me.

As I speed away, I look behind me into the glow of the garage that's slowly getting smaller and see Baylor bolting inside the cabin. I flick the lights on the front of my sled and race off into the mountain, feeling adrenaline coursing its way into my veins. I know this is stupid of me. Baylor is right; I shouldn't be out here, alone, in the dark. The white snow brightens the forest floor enough for me to see in front of me, but there are still a lot of shadows and trees that make my depth perception a little iffy. Not to mention, if I get stuck or fly off somewhere, I won't have anyone to help me.

I'll just stick to the route Henry took me on. That terrain wasn't too rough.

The cold air feels glorious, whipping through small pockets of my clothing. I didn't get a chance to really button down everything properly before I left, but I'm grateful to cool off and get my head straight.

I'm probably two miles away when I hear a faint zipping in the distance. I slow down to try to hear where it's coming from, and that's when I see a pair of lights from Henry's other sled coming over the hill. I recognize Baylor's jacket, and I grip the throttle hard, whipping up snow behind me as I take off in the opposite direction.

I glance back, seeing Baylor's sled quickly gaining on me. Damn it. That brief pause cost me.

Making a desperate decision, I give my sled some more gas as I veer down into the steep mountainside.

Baylor shouts something that sounds like a string of curse words, but my engine drowns him out. He hesitates at the top of the hill, and my thumb begins to ease off the throttle.

"Come on, Frost. Catch me," I mutter under my breath, looking back once more.

I can barely see him shaking his head before he finally plummets down the mountain after me.

My heart thumps in my chest, and I start laughing. I'm way off the course, and I have no idea where I am, but I don't care. I'd rather freeze to death or get trampled by a moose than let him catch me.

We weave back and forth for a few miles, creating fresh tracks in the snow. It's darker now, so when I can make out the sudden snowbank in front of me, it's too late to back out. My laughter stops when my snowmobile leaves the ground. I'm in the air for maybe two or three seconds before I hit the ground, but it feels like minutes. My body jerks forward, and I grunt as I take the impact of the landing. I hear Baylor's sled go through the air right after me and look back just in time to see him landing sideways.

"Shit!" I quickly turn back to head toward him. "Are you okay?" I yell, cutting off my engine.

Baylor crawls himself out from under the sled and manages to get to his feet. That's when I notice his boots are untied, he's still in his jeans, and his jacket isn't zipped up.

"What the hell is wrong with you?" He stomps toward me with purpose, brushing off snow stuck to his front.

"Is that rhetorical or—"

Suddenly, he's beside me. He reaches down and fists the front of my jacket, pulling me so I'm standing in front of him.

"Hey!"

"God-fucking-damn it, Aspen!" he yells, and I think he wants to hit me. "Do you have any idea how dangerous it is out here?"

I'm on my toes, my chest brushing his, but he's still towering over me with murderous eyes.

"What were you thinking, huh?" He tightens his fists and jerks me forward.

"I told you, I needed some goddamn air!" I shout up at him.

"Next time, step out onto the fucking deck or something! You don't go riding off into the dark on the side of a mountain!"

I grit my teeth together. "You didn't have to follow me! What, are you scared of what Henry would do if he found out you knew I'd left?"

"No, Aspen! Fuck!" He shakes his head, seething. "I'm scared of you not coming back! Why did you run off like that?"

His concern for me makes my chest tighten.

"I needed to get away from the house! Okay?" I swat at his chest, but he doesn't loosen his hold. "I needed …" I stop fighting him and look away, feeling weak. "I needed to get away from you."

After a few moments, he slowly lowers me and unravels his fists from my jacket. He doesn't speak. All I can hear in the silence of the snow are his heavy breaths.

"I don't understand what you're doing," I whisper, shaking my head. "You're mean to me. You're always mean to me."

"I know," he whispers.

"You referred to me as the help and practically threatened me in my bathroom the first night here, and then two days later, you were teaching me how to snowboard. You made sure my date stood me up, and then you kissed my shoulder and talked dirty in my ear the next day."

His expression is unreadable.

I sigh and look up at him. "I don't want to play your stupid games anymore, Baylor. You're screwing with my head, and I don't like it. If you hate me, you shouldn't be trying to get in my pants."

"I've never hated you," Baylor says, glancing down at my lips.

I let out a frustrated growl and push him away. "It's like you didn't hear a word I said, did you?"

His white teeth appear as a smile spreads across his face. "I heard you, Aspen."

"Whatever." I huff and climb back onto the snowmobile. "Let's get back then. I'll go slower so you can keep up this time."

Baylor walks over to his sled and pushes it upright. I wait for his engine to sound, but after a few seconds, I don't hear anything.

"What's wrong?"

He shrugs and tries it again. "Must've messed something up when I landed." His boots sink into the deep snow as he walks back over to me.

"Sucks to be you." I grin.

"What? Are you going to leave me out here?" He mocks me, as if he doesn't think I have that cold of a heart.

I raise my chin. "Maybe I will."

He shakes his head and laughs. "You wouldn't do that."

"Oh, I really don't think you're in a good position to be underestimating me." I squeeze the throttle and launch the sled forward a few feet, watching Baylor's smug grin fall from his face. As entertaining as it is, it's darker than I'm comfortable with, and I feel a little guilty that he followed me out here, looking the way he does. He's probably freezing. I'm still not even sure how far we've pushed each other out during our chase, so I give in and pat the seat behind me. "Alright, fine. Get on."

He quickly jumps on the back, like he's scared I might change my mind, and then wraps his arms around me. His hard body presses against mine in an alarmingly erotic way. I can feel his stomach flexing on my back with every slow breath he takes. His firm, long legs trap me in a Baylor cage. And that's exactly what I am—trapped between a wall of hard muscle and machine.

"I can drive if you want," he offers.

"Not a chance." Driving the sled is the one shred of control I feel I have left here.

His biceps contract around my rib cage, giving me a squeeze to let me know he's ready, and I gently push on the gas. The temperatures dropped quickly after the sun went down, so I welcome the protection and warmth Baylor gives me.

As I head back up the mountain, I start to recognize where I am and realize we went out a lot farther than I thought we did. I ask him for directions on a few turns I'm unsure of, but every time he adjusts his hold on me, my breathing gets heavier.

"You okay?" he asks, tilting his head.

I stiffen and nod. Maybe if I just don't move or breathe or think, I'll make it back to the cabin without him knowing how much he's affecting me right now.

Baylor moves one arm lower and one higher, tightening his hold on me.

The muscles in my abdomen tremble.

His chin rests on my shoulder, right next to my neck. "There's something you should know, Penny."

I inhale slowly. *Three … two … one.* "Yeah? What's that?"

"I didn't offer Shaun the amount of money Henry said I did."

I ease off the gas a bit so I can hear him better. "What are you talking about?"

He exhales with what sounds like frustration. "I didn't think a couple of hundred would work on him, so I handed him about two grand and told him if he showed up at Heights, he wouldn't like what happened to him."

I stare out at the snow-covered path in front of me, letting his words soak in. But the more I run the scenario through my head, the more I can hear my pulse in my ears. My cheeks ignite first and then my whole body. I'm not sure if that reaction is out of anger or something else. "Why would you do that? Is my humiliation worth that much to you?"

"No," he tells me. His hands move again, and I think he's removing his gloves. "Because no one is touching you on this trip if it isn't me."

My lips part, and I suck in a breath.

*What?*

His teeth drag up the sensitive slope of my neck. "Are you still convinced I hate you? You think I didn't want to bend your naked body over that sink the first night?"

My breath turns ragged.

"I've never seen anything more beautiful than when you were soaking wet, standing in front of me like that. Fuck. The things I've dreamed of doing to you every day since then."

My first instinct is to ask what they are, but I swallow back that curiosity.

"You're lying," I say. Because nothing makes sense if it's true.

"The only lie is if you believe I just started fantasizing about you since you got here. I've thought about having you all to myself, every which way, every day since I met you, Aspen. Making you angry with me is just a bonus." His lips are below my ear when he says, "Because the way you glare at me from across a room makes my cock hard." He rolls his hips into my ass, and I feel it.

I bite my lip hard to keep from moaning at the images forcing their way into my head. But it escapes the moment he attaches his mouth to the nape of my neck and sucks. As soon as he releases, the cold air hits the wetness and sends a shiver down my spine.

"There's no one out here, Aspen. We could just stop the sled right here, in the middle of the woods. It could be our little secret if you want. I'll keep you warm."

He slides a hand under my jacket. His cold fingers are a shock to my system at first, but then he's teasing the skin below my bra, and I'm wet. The other hand wanders lower, cupping me from the outside.

"Stop the sled, Aspen."

Stopping would make everything real right now, so I shake my head even though the tiny pulse between my legs is begging me to say yes.

He applies pressure to where I want it most, and my hips roll forward.

"Your hatred for me turns you on, doesn't it?"

The hand inside my shirt pushes my bra up and cups my breast.

"Fuck," he rasps. "They're so soft and perfect. Made just for my hands. My mouth."

"Baylor," I start to protest, but his name is barely audible when the pad of his thumb brushes my nipple.

"Do you want me to touch you, Aspen?" He asks for permission in the sultriest of voices as his fingers tease the waistline of my pants.

I want to shake my head and stop him, but I want this so much more.

My lip trembles, and I nod.

He skillfully undoes the button with one hand and slides it along my skin—beneath the snow pants, the waistline of my leggings, and the thin layer of lace panties.

My mouth drops open with an uneven breath when his first finger finds my clit.

"Aspen." He grits out my name as he starts to rub circles.

"Baylor," I whimper.

He uses his pointer finger and ring finger to spread my lips and works his middle finger through my center at a faster pace. "Do you like this?"

I nod, too delirious for words.

He dips the tips of his fingers into my entrance and immediately returns to my clit. "You have no idea how bad I wish it were my mouth making you feel this way right now."

My bundle of nerves is hit over and over and over. I have to tighten my grip on the handlebars for support. We shoot forward, faster, and Baylor's circles on my sensitive flesh get smaller and quicker.

"Oh my—" I'm panting. Losing control. My finger slips off the gas, and Baylor's fingers practically seize. "No, please—" I beg. "Don't stop."

Baylor kisses the spot just below my ear and whispers, "You're driving this, baby."

Through the lust-filled dizziness, I register what he tells me and slowly ease back on the throttle.

Baylor continues kneading my breast as he slides one finger inside me. Then two. Stretching me little by little. The heel of his hand applies pressure in a glorious rhythm as he pumps me to the speed I command him to.

Faster.

Deeper.

We enter a clearing in the forest, and I accelerate across the flat, snow-covered opening.

"That's my girl," Baylor says, burying his face in my neck. He slides a third finger in easily and works his hand until my thighs are shaking.

I throw my head back on his chest and roll my hips forward into his hand. Slowly at first and then in sharp thrusts.

"You can take whatever you want with me. Be greedy, baby. I beg you."

Every muscle in my body is on fire, and my pulse is pounding like a hammer.

My whimpers turn into tiny screams as I feel the tension pooling in my core.

Baylor growls something into my neck, releasing some willpower, and he nudges my ass with his thick erection.

I exhale hard, climbing and waiting.

He grunts as he thrusts into me from behind while I fuck his hand. It's a dance I never want to end, but as my orgasm crests, I can barely take much more.

I manage to accelerate the sled forward a fraction, and it's all I need. "Baylor, I'm—"

"Let go. No one will hear you but me," Baylor says.

He gently pinches my nipple, and I shatter.

Warmth explodes over my whole body. I cry out his name, but it's lost in the wind. Baylor's movements become softer as I ride out the rest of the wave, savoring the electric current humming beneath my skin. When our breathing evens out a bit, he removes his hands and takes over the controls of the snowmobile. I collapse back into his chest.

A few minutes later, I see the twinkling glow of Christmas lights come into view as we round the back of the cabin. I'm glad at least one of us has a sense of direction because both my internal and moral compasses are out of order.

All of a sudden, we're in the garage. Baylor climbs off the back of the sled and looks over at the door to the house like he's afraid someone will come through it and discover us. I'm not sure how long we've been gone, but I'd guess Henry, Jesse, or Luke would've noticed we were missing by now.

Cold winter air whistles through the garage and hits my back, waking me up. My head clears, giving me flashes of a night that will haunt my dreams from here on out.

"Wh … what did we just do?" I mutter.

I'm trying to think if there were any frozen lakes I passed on my slutty little adventure that would be thin enough to fall into when I notice the large and painful-looking bulge in Baylor's pants. My cheeks turn a shade of red you'd be able to spot from space.

His hand grazes my cheek, and he smiles down at me like he knows one of my dirty secrets.

*Holy fuck.*

Baylor Frost just became my dirtiest secret of all.

"Please don't overthink this, Penny. Every word I said to you tonight was the truth. Do with that what you will, okay? I can wait."

# 7

# NO, ASPEN. BAD ASPEN.

This isn't how my break was supposed to go. The plan was to come to Aspen and spend a quiet Christmas with Henry and Clara. Not to have Baylor give me one of the best orgasms of my life on the back of a fucking snowmobile.

When I got back to my room last night, I tried to shower off the twisting thoughts still lingering in the forefront of my mind. I lathered up my loofah and began scrubbing away Baylor's touch, but the loofah quickly became Baylor's hands again, and I found my second release of the night. My vanilla body wash is very fragrant, so I'm pretty sure my vagina smells like a frickin' sugar cookie now.

I was dreading facing Baylor so much this morning that I couldn't muster up the courage to go downstairs or even get out of bed, which made my head spiral with scenarios I know would never happen. One of which was Henry finding out about us and never speaking to me again. I know he wouldn't do that. He probably wouldn't even care. But that dark corner of my mind that's constantly going through what-ifs makes me believe anything is possible.

The other scenario, which seems more accurate, was that this was really just another one of Baylor's ways of torturing me, and now, everyone downstairs already knows every juicy detail about our affair last night.

This wasn't like when he saw me naked. The way he looked at me then made me feel powerful and desirable. No, this was different. Baylor has all of the power now. How could he not after unraveling me the way he did?

Knuckles rap on my door, and my heart jumps into my throat.

*Stop thinking about him.*

"Aspen?" Henry's voice calls from the other side of the door, and I relax a little. "Dinner will be ready soon."

"I'm just getting ready," I respond, tying the straps of my dress around my neck.

"Don't feel like you have to push yourself if you're still not feeling up for it. I can always bring you a plate to eat up here instead."

A pang of guilt hits me. I told Henry my head was hurting, and that's why I've been in my room all day. It was a partial truth; my head did start to hurt at one point from all the overthinking.

"No, no. I'm okay. I'll be just a minute."

Silence falls between us, but I know he's still there.

"Hey, Pen?"

I frown, glancing back at the door. "Mmhmm?"

"Baylor and I went and retrieved the other sled this morning."

I swallow hard.

"He said you went out there all by yourself?"

"I know it was dangerous. I shouldn't have."

"Why would you do that? You know I would've taken you out if you'd asked me to. Did something happen?"

I release a nervous laugh. "I just wanted to get out of the house. You know, fresh powder 'n' all."

I hear him laugh.

"I didn't think it'd be that big of a deal. I'm sorry."

"It's okay. I'm glad Baylor followed you."

*Me too.*

"You could've been hurt."

"Well, I'm fine."

"I know. I guess I should be more concerned with Baylor riding since he's the one who took a spill."

"Did you get it working again?"

"Oh, yeah, we got it working just fine. I'm not sure what happened to it out there."

I ponder on that for a moment. Baylor could've easily fooled me into believing his snowmobile wasn't working just to ride back with me. Did I think to check it? No.

"By the way, those guys who are here … they've been into the whiskey pretty heavily. Just, um, try to ignore anything stupid they might say, okay?" His words are laced with regret. "I'm sorry in advance."

His footsteps fade down the hallway, away from my door, and I'm immediately filled with unease. Not that I wasn't before, but something about his tone nearly tips me over the edge.

I consider Henry's offer of bringing my dinner up to my room so I can barricade myself in here until this trip is over when I get another look at myself in the mirror.

I am *glowing*.

My makeup is minimal, which only makes me more impressed with the smoothness of my skin and the brightness of my eyes. A pretty rose shade lip oil makes my lips look full and plump. I went through the trouble of fastening my hair into a braided updo with a few dainty blonde tendrils framing my face, but I think I chose a more difficult hairstyle to occupy my mind.

I shouldn't waste this, right?

I take a deep breath and shake my sweaty palms out at my sides.

*Okay. I can do this. I'm ready to face the ridicule. The judgment. Baylor.*

*Fuck.* The second I'm reminded of him, my insides flutter.

*Chin up, Aspen. Do this for yourself. If anything, you're the one who at least got an orgasm out of all of this. Not him. So, the joke is really on him, right?*

I grab the bottom of my black satin dress, lifting it up so I don't trip on the extra fabric around the hem, and march out of my room before I change my mind.

Various deep voices echo up into the hallway from the main floor—some I recognize, some I don't.

As I round the corner to the staircase, I glance at the small crowd of men below me, drinking and laughing. Henry and an older gentleman are smoking cigars and appear to be in a serious conversation while Jesse and Luke are almost in tears, chatting with the other two men.

Liquid warmth pools in my stomach when I spot Baylor standing directly in the middle of the living room by himself, holding a half-empty glass in one hand while his other casually rests in his pocket. He looks bored and unimpressed, per usual, but also effortlessly sexy in his perfect white shirt and black trousers.

As if he feels me there, his eyes rise and lock on to mine, nearly knocking the wind out of my lungs. I quickly look away to focus on the stairs so I don't trip, but his gaze has a weight to it, and I can feel it with every move I make, every step I get closer to him.

When I step off the landing, he's already there, blocking my path.

The corner of my mouth pulls up when I notice that the crisp white shirt stretching over his hard chest is the same one I wore to bed my first night here.

I reach up to touch the Armani logo on his collar when he snatches my wrist out of the air. My eyes widen as they shoot to him.

"You look fucking gorgeous. Now, for the love of God, go upstairs and change," he says, but it sounds more like an order.

I look down at my dress and back up at his pained expression. "Hmm, no."

"Please," he says through clenched teeth.

I yank my wrist out of his grasp and blink up at him. "And what would you propose I wear instead?"

"Anything else. I don't care." He shakes his head firmly.

"Well, I left my burlap sack at home, and Henry told me to wear something nice. This is the only dress I packed, other than that sweater dress." I smile, knowing he remembers the one.

His nostrils flare. "Aspen, you don't know these guys. I can't rearrange their faces if they look at you the wrong way. They work with Henry's father."

I slide my hands up the seam of his shirt and undo the top button, feeling more powerful with every pleading word he breathes.

"I'm asking you one more time to please change." He's not demanding me anymore; he's begging.

With heels on, I'm closer to his face, but I still have to rise up onto my tiptoes to reach his ear. "Make me," I whisper, grazing my lips along his earlobe.

I start to push past him, but he catches me by the throat and pulls me back in front of him. His hold on me is soft yet firm enough to elicit a moan from me.

"You know I can."

My legs are unsteady beneath me as my whole body pulses. His dominance and protectiveness complement his anger in the best way, making my thighs ache.

"Aspen?" Jesse utters my name from the other side of Baylor.

Baylor drops his hand and reluctantly steps aside.

Jesse looks between the two of us, making sure I'm okay, and then pins Baylor with a death glare. "You've resorted to putting your hands on her? Are you insane?"

Baylor smirks down at me and whispers, "You didn't seem to mind last night."

I swallow hard, unsure if I want to pummel him or kiss him.

*Kiss him? No, Aspen. Bad Aspen.*

Jesse's frown deepens as he takes a step toward Baylor. "What'd he fucking say to you?"

I've never seen him worked up like this. He's usually so calm and happy. This version of Jesse is kind of scary.

"It's fine, Jesse." I sigh, relieved that he doesn't seem to know anything about what happened last night. "Baylor and I just had a … disagreement."

"Yeah, sure. Whatever." He still looks like he's ready to murder his friend when he puts an arm over my shoulders and leads me into the dining room. "You look nice, by the way," he says after a beat.

"That's a generous adjective, coming from you." I grin. "Thank you."

"Well, well, well. You *do* have some female companions to keep us entertained tonight, Donner." A large, middle-aged man in an expensive suit eyes me up as he takes a puff from his cigar.

Henry winces, just a few steps behind him, but I expected something like this.

"Is it just the one?" The man looks around the room. "Well then, I guess we'll have to share, won't we?"

"Aspen Holly. Nice to meet you …" I extend my hand, waiting for him to introduce himself.

He looks down at my hand and laughs, shoving his free hand in his pants pocket.

*Prick.*

He blows smoke up into the ceiling before speaking. "The name's Rollins, sweetheart. But you can call me King."

Yeah, I'm not going to do that. "Pleasure, I'm sure."

"Aspen, this is Peter and Jamie." Henry steps forward and gestures to the other two.

I don't bother holding out my hand this time. I just force a smile and nod at each of them.

"Aspen is a friend of mine who goes to Columbia with us," Henry adds.

"And what are you going for, Miss Holly?" Peter asks, adjusting his glasses as he drags his eyes away from my breasts.

"Psychology," I say.

"That's an interesting degree to choose." Peter nods.

Rollins chuckles. "Worthless, if you ask me."

I don't hesitate. "I could say the same thing about your hairline."

The room falls silent.

I'm scared to see what kind of face Henry is giving me, so I maintain eye contact with the entitled asshole who decided to share his opinion with me when I hadn't asked for it.

Jesse and Luke snicker, which causes the rest of the men to burst out laughing, and the tension in the air dissipates.

Jamie's squinty eyes brighten. "I like this one. She's feisty."

Rollins pats his belly and grunts as he walks around the dining table and takes a seat at the very end. I can't help but notice it's the farthest away from me.

We all sit down and quickly start passing around plates of food. Marta went all out for tonight. Roasted pear salad, prime rib, garlic and rosemary potatoes, caviar with crème fraiche, sautéed asparagus, and more that hasn't reached my end of the table yet.

I focus on loading up my plate while the guys talk business and whatever else. It's easy for me to zone out their conversation after my first few bites.

I peek up at Baylor as he spears the meat on his plate and brings it to his mouth. There's something sensual about the way he chews that makes the world around me slow. My gaze is fixed on his lips when he leisurely wets it with his tongue. I drag my eyes up to meet his and inhale sharply.

His tense brows and dark stare are set on me in a scowl-like expression, but a smile softens his eyes when he flicks his gaze down to my lips.

*You look really pretty*, Baylor mouths.

My cheeks flush as I smile back.

Silverware clink against our empty plates as we finish up dinner, and we all thank Marta for the meal. Well, most of us. I'm not surprised when Rollins looks inconvenienced when she goes to clear his plate from the table.

Henry touches my arm and leans in. "Did I say how sorry I was yet?"

"Don't worry about it, Henry." I thread my fingers through his and give him a reassuring squeeze.

"Aye now. Don't go picking favorites just yet, princess. You haven't seen my handsome poker face." Jamie raises a brow and tries making a sultry face, but it just sends a shiver up my spine in a slimy way.

"Welp." Henry stands, blocking the others' view of me. "Shall we go play some cards, gentlemen?"

"Are you in a hurry to be annihilated again, Donner?" Peter asks before tossing the rest of his drink back.

"I'm always interested in taking your daddy's money." Rollins smirks as he struggles out of his seat.

I see Henry's fists clench at his sides, but he stays calm, like always, and leads everyone downstairs into the billiard room.

My eyes close, and I soak in the silence. I didn't realize my heart was beating so fast until it was quiet enough to hear it. After a few deep breaths and sips of my drink, I feel clear-minded enough to get up.

Marta catches me as she comes out of the kitchen, offering an extra apron and a sweet smile. "I'm going to make some cookies. Do you want to help?"

I'm elated. I've spent enough time in my room today, and I wasn't the least bit tired.

We spend the next couple of hours mixing batter, rolling out dough, and shaping cookies. The house is filled with the aroma of freshly baked cookies—probably more than anyone can eat—and I only have a dusting of flour on the side of my dress. Impressive.

After eating a cookie—or four—I shed my apron, dust myself off, and head downstairs to see how the game is going.

The air has a smoky haze to it as I enter the room. Henry's resting his head in both of his hands as Baylor throws his cards down on the table, folding.

Rollins lets out a deep belly laugh as Henry quickly turns over his cards like he's ripping off a Band-Aid.

"Fuck," Henry shouts.

"Maybe you should go back to playing Go Fish, boy," Rollins quips as he rounds up the chips in the pot.

Luke must be dealing because he starts shuffling the deck for a new game.

"I almost had you," Jesse says, shaking his head. "I think I'm out, guys."

I see the defeat on Henry's face and decide to have some fun.

"Hello, boys." I saunter over to the round wooden table. "Who's winning?" I bat my eyes at Rollins, already knowing the answer from the massive pile of chips in front of him.

Rollins raises his chin. "That'd be me, sweetheart."

Baylor swivels his head to look at me, and I do my best to ignore him. Something tells me he's not going to like this.

"You want a drink, Aspen?" Jesse offers.

"Please," I reply, looking around the table to see how everyone is doing.

Jamie and Baylor seem to be doing okay but have nearly half of what Rollins has. Peter runs his fingers through his last stack of chips but looks to be pretty optimistic. And Henry is almost out.

"Hey, princess!" Jamie waves a hand at me. "Bring that ass over here so I can rub it for good luck."

I watch the muscles in Baylor's bicep flex beneath his shirt.

The chair behind me creaks before a smack ensues.

Baylor is out of his chair before I even feel the fire on my ass cheek.

I have to bite back the instinct to give Peter the same sting across his face tenfold. Though, from the looks of it, Baylor has plans to do much worse to my assailant.

I crane my head and look at Peter. He has his hands in the air, like Baylor has a weapon drawn on him.

"Oh, come on. He's just a little drunk and having some fun." The cigar in Rollins's mouth bobs as he speaks.

I give Henry a look across the table and nod.

He raises a brow and fights back a smile. "Want us to deal you in, Pen?"

I shrug. "Why not?"

# 8

# FLUSHED

"Do you even know the rules of the game, sweetheart?" Rollins is quick to question.

"Is it the same as strip poker?" I scrunch my nose, playing dumb. "I played that at a friend's house one time, but I was terrible!"

"Jesus." Henry rakes a hand down his face.

Rollins, Peter, and Jamie all exchange glances of amusement.

"Aspen!" Baylor grits out my name.

"What? You guys have been down here for hours, and I'm bored." I pout.

"Yeah, let her have some fun, Frost." Rollins winks at me.

Jesse sets a wine glass down in front of me, and I thank him.

"Can she even afford the buy-in?" Peter asks, looking around the table.

Jamie tips his whiskey glass at me. "Yeah, this isn't your college party kind of stakes, princess."

"I'll stake her." Henry shrugs.

"You're bleeding chips, Donner. Let me cover for you," Rollins says.

I smile. "I think I'll go with Henry. I know he's good for it."

Rollins almost chokes on his next breath. "Girl, I'm the richest man in this room."

"And the humblest, I see," I retort.

Henry laughs, and I'm glad to see his spirit has changed.

"I'll still stick with Henry's offer in case I need to pay him back."

Rollins raises a suggestive brow. "I have better ways you can pay off your debt that don't involve cash."

I instinctively put my hand on Baylor's thigh beneath the table. He covers my hand with his and rubs a thumb over my knuckles. "Maybe you can help me with my first hand?" I ask him.

He frowns down at me. "Aspen, I really don't think this is a good idea."

"Don't worry. I'm a fast learner." I bite my lip and smile and then raise my voice for the rest of the table. "I mean, how hard can it be, right?"

"Looks like I'm going home with the deepest pockets tonight, boys." Rollins holds a finger up to signal to Jesse for another pour.

"I like your confidence, Aspen," Luke tells me. He slides me my chips and then starts dealing.

"Can we at least lower the blind until she plays a few rounds?" Henry asks.

"Sure thing." Jamie nods in agreement.

"You want a slower beating, huh?" Rollins chuckles.

Henry rolls his eyes.

Peter looks down at his cards, worry etched between his two fluffy brows. "Just so we're clear, we're keeping our clothes on, right?"

Well, damn. His poker face is terrible.

Rollins scowls. "What do you think, imbecile?"

Baylor leans over so he can see my cards, and I breathe in his scent. It's warm and woodsy. He looks down at my hand and gives me a quick rundown of what the best cards are to have and why. He's patient and concise. It'd be constructive for a beginner, and I smile at that.

My first hand is trash, but instead of listening to Baylor and folding as I should, I raise.

"Raise!" I shout, throwing a red chip into the pot. "I've always wanted to do that."

Baylor lowers his chin and mutters, "What the hell?"

"That's three grand, princess," Jamie says. "You sure about that?"

*Three fucking grand?*

I swallow hard but keep the smile on my face. "Mmhmm!"

"Call," Peter says.

Henry scans my face and smiles. "Call."

"Call." Rollins nods.

"Fucking call, I guess." Baylor shakes his head and throws in a chip to match me.

Three hands later, I finally fold my losing hand. I try to convince myself the chips are ones and fives, but everyone keeps shouting their raises and reminding me how much Henry's money is sitting at my fingertips.

Baylor is furious with me, so I shrug him off and tell him I don't need his help. His realization is going to be so much sweeter than I thought.

My next deal is the high card, and I can't help but play it through to get my chips back. I fold my next two hands immediately even though one of them is a straight, just to watch the rest of the table.

Peter is an easy tell. Everything is written all over his face the moment he looks at his cards. He is just quick to conceal it.

Jamie takes a long drink from his glass when he has a bad hand. It gives him more time to ponder the stakes and consider his next move.

Henry is harder to read, but he hates losing, so he doesn't bet big unless he knows he's got the highest hand. That habit hasn't changed since the first time I played him.

Baylor is actually a pretty good player. He won a round with nothing, just by upping the ante more than the rest of the table was comfortable with. He takes risks and has a stone-cold face with zero tells. I think, right now, the only thing distracting him is me. He doesn't want to lose, but he also doesn't want to beat me. If I were really playing against him, I'd use that. But I'm not. I'm here to humiliate Henry's company and leave them with empty pockets.

Rollins is a tricky one, so I study him the closest. Lucky for me, he's playing like he never loses. That's mistake number one. His second mistake is drinking as much as he has; his decision-making is hazy at best. And his third is underestimating the innocent blonde sitting across from him.

Luke deals a new hand, and I feel the adrenaline kick in. I'm done playing stupid.

I get pocket fours, which turns into a full house—the highest hand this round.

"Psh, that was lucky," Rollins grumbles.

Jesse narrows his eyes at me from the bar and tips the corner of his mouth up slightly.

I throw back the rest of my drink and get ready for the next hand.

Jamie and Peter are convinced they have the better hand and blindly up the ante every round. They've already ruled out the rest of the table, and they're playing each other like it's a pissing contest.

Rollins and Baylor fold and Henry soon after.

"She's got nothin'." Jamie drops his eyes from me and glances at his hand for the fourteenth time.

Peter is getting worse at hiding his enthusiasm with each finger of bourbon he polishes off and makes his worst decision of the night. "I'm all in, fellas."

Jamie shakes his head at his colleague and calls, pushing his tower of chips in with Peter's.

The room is silent as they all wait for me to take the final move.

I call too.

Peter is already reaching for the money in the center of the table after Jamie lays down a lower hand than his, and then I lay down mine.

Peter freezes.

"This is good, right?" I tilt my head.

Henry eyes me with an amused expression on his face.

"Holy shit," Jesse says.

"A ROYAL FUCKING FLUSH?" Luke erupts.

Jamie's jaw nearly unhinges. "You had that this whole time?"

"You hustled us." Baylor's mouth tightens into a prideful grin.

"You bitch! You fucking bitch!" Peter points an angry finger at me.

"Aye! Watch it!" Baylor snaps.

Rollins slams a fist on the table. "Is this your idea of a good time, Donner? Bringing a shark to a friendly game of poker?"

"This hasn't been a friendly game from the moment you all disrespected her," Henry tells him.

Rollins scoffs. "I didn't come here to be hustled by some blonde whore you dragged out here to pass around to all of your friends."

Glasses clink behind the bar as Jesse shouts, "Hey!"

"Speak to her like that again, and I'll rip your fucking tongue out," Baylor snarls.

Henry gives Baylor a look.

Rollins laughs at what he thinks is a futile threat until Baylor rises from his seat. His ego slowly diminishes. "Fine. We'll take our money and go. Don't think I won't fill your father in on this little trick you played, Donner."

I'm torn between letting him go and finishing what I started.

"Are you saying I didn't beat you fairly?" I ask teasingly.

Rollins pauses from his leave. "Don't test me, girl. It wasn't an honorable game, and you know it."

"Why? Because you lost?"

He purses his lips. "Listen here, sweetheart. They call me King because I'm the king of poker. I don't lose. So, the fact that you depleted me of half my chips can only mean one thing: I was cheated."

"Bull-fucking-shit!" Henry shouts.

"She beat you fair and square, old man," Luke adds.

I lean forward, eyeing him. "What do you say you and I play a game of honor then?"

"I don't need to win back my money to prove anything. If for some reason you beat me, I still won't lose. I'm filthy rich, sweetheart!"

"Let's not play for just the money then," I say.

He lifts a bored brow at my proposal.

"Whoever has the lower hand loses a layer of clothing."

Baylor's head whips to me, making the butterflies come alive in my stomach.

"We play until there are no layers left."

Rollins throws his head back and howls. "That's absurd. Why on earth would I do that?"

Everyone looks at me.

I nod at the giant pile of poker chips in the pot. "Winner takes all."

"Pen …" Henry says warily.

Rollins's eyes narrow. He's considering it, but he's not convinced.

I release a small laugh. "Don't tell me you haven't pictured me naked since I introduced myself to you upstairs."

There's a rumble from Baylor's throat as Rollins drags his eyes down my front.

"Besides, you already have the upper hand, *King*." The name tastes sour on my tongue.

"How's that?" he asks.

"I don't have very many layers on."

That seals the deal.

Rollins threads his arms through his sport coat to add an extra layer, sits back in his chair, and lights a fresh cigar. "Deal us in."

Luke's face lights up as he shuffles the deck and starts the first round.

Baylor leaves my side and moves about the room, watching from afar.

My opponent still seems a bit on edge, so I throw my first hand as a confidence booster to him, and I lose my heels.

"Those shouldn't count!" Peter protests.

I chuck my shoes at him, and Jamie scrambles to claim them for himself.

My next three hands cause Rollins to shed his coat, shoes, and socks. But I try not to get too cocky. His focus has increased, making him harder for me to read.

My spirit shakes when I'm dealt a set of aces, and Rollins surprises me with two pairs.

The room is silent when I lay down my cards, waiting.

I stand and find Baylor in the corner, watching me as I untie my dress and let it fall to the ground.

The room explodes with a string of whistles, but all I can hear is my heartbeat as I watch Baylor's pupils dilate.

Rollins blows smoke at me as I sit back down in just my strapless lace bra and high-rise panties. "Two more."

"So, it's just been the four of you and her up here, in the mountains?" Jamie murmurs in the background.

Out of the corner of my eye, I see Henry smack him upside the head, and I try not to laugh.

I take Rollins hand after hand over the next hour until he's down to his plaid boxers.

"I really thought you'd be more of a briefs kind of guy," I sneer.

"Give us our damn cards, boy," Rollins barks at Luke and taps the table.

The guys snicker quietly to themselves.

My two kings I'm dealt get me three of a kind, but I have a sneaky suspicion Rollins has a pair in his hand too. Mine might be higher, but if he's got nines, off my bra goes.

And as much as I hate to admit it, the only person in this room I'm removing my bra for is going to be Baylor.

I resist the urge to look up at him.

The air is thick with suspense, and it feels like all eight of us are holding our breath together as Luke flips the last card over. A wave of relief washes over me when I see it's another king.

Rollins smiles and slams his cards down. "Let's see those tits, sweetheart. Kings and nines! Full house!"

*I knew it.*

"Aspen?" Luke signals to me.

I hold on to Rollins's gaze for a moment longer, wanting to witness every wrinkle and frown line get deeper as he realizes he just lost.

"You can keep those on." I nod at the only article of clothing he has left and place my cards on the table.

Four kings—a higher hand.

"Damn, Pen! Four of a kind!" Henry claps. "You didn't have that until the last card?"

I shake my head.

"No fucking way!" Jamie stands and leans over the table for a better view.

Rollins stares at my cards in denial for a long while.

Luke drops to one knee at my side. "Will you fucking marry me?"

"No, me! Marry me, Aspen!" Jesse pushes him over and takes his place. "I'm better in the sack than he is."

My hand covers my heart. "Such romantic gestures."

"Get up, idiots." Henry chuckles before coming in to congratulate me. He gives me an awkward one-armed hug because, well, I'm almost naked.

I offer Rollins a handshake, which he actually accepts.

"Not bad, sweetheart. Not bad."

My grip on his hand tightens. "It's Aspen. Not sweetheart."

"Aspen," he corrects, and I let go.

I glance around the room at the excitement and celebration and realize Baylor's nowhere to be seen. He left, but I'm not sure when—or why.

"I'm going to go shower and put some clothes on, okay?" I tell Henry, gathering my shoes and my dress up in my arms.

"Yeah, of course. I'll take care of everything down here."

I head up to my room, taking a roundabout route to check the rooms on the main floor. I pause when I reach the hallway to my bedroom and see Baylor pacing just outside my door. *There he is.*

"Baylor?"

He stops in his tracks and looks up at me through a veil of desperation.

"Are you all right?" I search his face, feeling a strange sensation in my chest.

His breathing turns shallow, like he's in pain. Then, it's as if something snaps in his head. His willpower? His sanity?

In three strides, Baylor has his body pressed against mine. Cradling the back of my head, he spins me and slams me up against the wall.

I open my mouth in surprise, and he kisses me hard, darting his tongue between my parted lips.

There's a longing in the way he claims me. He's biting at my lips and stroking his hot tongue against mine, hungry and wild. It's like he's finally been set free from restraints he's grown too familiar with. He doesn't know how to control his assault.

From the throbbing between my legs, I don't think I mind his chaotic kisses. I like them so much that I wrap my arms around his middle, push off the wall, and trade places with him.

He grunts and then smiles lazily against my lips. "I've been dying to do this all night."

"You have?" I ask between kisses.

His forearm presses into my lower back, bringing me even closer. "I've never been so turned on while losing money."

I reach up and fist his hair as he releases a husky moan into my mouth.

"Aspen, you forgot—"

I jump back from Baylor when I hear Henry's voice coming toward us.

"Your phone," he slowly finishes, looking at the two of us.

There's no hiding or denying what he just walked in on. I'm panting and flushed, and Baylor's shirt is hanging open.

*When did I do that?*

I can't read Henry's expression to know what he's thinking. He doesn't look angry. Or surprised. Or even disgusted. It's like a tiny wheel is spinning in his head as he processes everything.

After a beat, Henry lifts his arm and hands me my phone.

I snatch it nervously. "Thank you."

Baylor draws in a breath and tilts his head back against the wall behind him, staring up at the ceiling.

Henry nods steadily, still switching his gaze from me to Baylor.

I hook my thumb over my shoulder. "I'm just going to, um …" I'm turning the handle to my room before I finish.

My chest heaves as my back hits the door.

I don't know what that kiss was, but it felt … good. Better than good. It felt *right*.

# 9

# MORE THAN EVER

It's four in the morning on Christmas Day, and I'm wide awake. Torn from a fitful sleep by a naughty dream, I wander downstairs to find something to keep my mind occupied.

My bare feet pad across the kitchen floor as I search for a late-night—er, morning—snack. It's a habitual routine I turn to when I can't fall back asleep.

The cold air feels good against my bare legs in comparison to the warmth of my room. My body was on fire after I woke up from my dream. I turned on my fan and threw the duvet off the bed, but I still couldn't stop burning up.

I take a glass out of the cupboard and fill it with ice-cold water, lift it to my lips, and empty it in a few gulps as I stare out the kitchen window. Snow gently falls to the ground, sparkling from a moonlit sky. It's a peaceful image, and after a while, I can feel my muscles relax and my pulse slow.

Being as quiet as I can, I gather some fruit and cheese from the refrigerator and a cutting board from a drawer, and I put together a mini charcuterie board for myself. I bite down on a grape when the fridge light beams across the kitchen. I jerk my head around and see Baylor reaching for an apple out of the drawer.

"Jesus. You scared me," I tell him in a hushed tone.

He closes the door, returning the kitchen to its darkened state, and looks at me. The soft glow of the moon shining through the window is like a spotlight highlighting his naked torso. The muscles on his stomach tighten as he lets out a small laugh.

"What?"

"Couldn't sleep either?" he asks. He brings the apple up to his mouth and bites down, wiping the juice from his lips with the back of his hand.

My mouth waters at the sight.

Baylor rolls his eyes down the front of my tank top as he chews.

The points of my breasts pebble beneath his stare.

He smiles when he sees them, raising a brow. "Penny?"

I quickly turn my back to him and shake my head. "Why do you call me that?" I ask, frustrated.

"Because you get this cute little crease between your eyebrows when I do."

*Well, fuck.* Why did that just make my heart thrash against my chest?

I hear him advance across the room, his steps getting closer, and I grab the handle of the knife beside me.

The metal blade sings as I slide it across the cutting board and raise it toward his throat in warning. "Don't."

He stops where he is, but he's already so close that I can feel his warmth. His eyes lower to the tip of the knife but then continue down the edge and to the handle I'm white-knuckling before dancing up my shoulder to my collarbone.

My grip loosens.

I can feel the heat from his stare lingering on my neck. And then with heavy eyelids, his gaze slowly finds my lips, and I immediately inhale because the tension has seized all the oxygen from my lungs. I feel his hand over mine, taking the knife from me. He lays it back down beside me and continues closing the small distance left between us. It's not far, but I wish I had an extra inch to think. To process. To create an avoidance plan. To *breathe*. To—

"You're trying to come up with more reasons to despise me than to be with me," Baylor tells me. "But you're failing, aren't you? You're attracted to me—that much is obvious—but there's more. You like the way I fight with you. The way I challenge you."

The hand that put the knife down is pressing on my hip, guiding me backward into the island, while his other curls around my neck.

"The way I touch you," he says.

His thumb and thick pointer finger are firm at my jaw as he tilts my head back to make my mouth more accessible to him while the rest of his hold is gentle, longing.

"You like the way I make you feel."

"Baylor," I breathe out, trying to muster up the ability to push him away. But for some reason, my arms don't want to move.

Then, the realization hits me like a punch to the stomach. There's no part of me that wants to push him away. He's right. I want … him. I want Baylor. Is that so bad?

Our noses touch.

"Go on, baby. Tell me how much you hate me," he whispers against my lips.

My resolve slips. "How about I show you?"

I curl my hand around the base of his neck and pull his mouth down to mine. My back arches against the counter as he comes down on me, his kiss hard and demanding. I hate that I want this, but I also think that's why it feels so damn good.

His tongue dives in, sweet and hot, determined to obliterate any reservations I have still gripping my sanity. I completely let go and submit to the desire fueling my movements.

There's a rumble in his throat as I slide my hands over the hard muscles of his chest. One of his legs slides between mine, parting them. I grind against it, my pulsing clit desperate to be touched.

His lips break away long enough for him to mutter a curse, and then he's on my neck, gliding his tongue along the soft skin. I let my neck fall to the side to give him better access and stifle a moan.

"You're going to have to be quiet, Aspen. I don't mind announcing to the whole house that I finally have you, but I don't think you want that."

I bite my lip as his hands run down the front of my body, pausing to palm my breasts over the thin fabric.

His grin widens, and his emerald eyes pierce mine. "I hope you're not too attached to this."

"Wh-what?" I stutter.

His hands meet at the top of my tank and tear it right down the middle like it's nothing. I'm about to scold him when he bends down and takes my hardened peak in his mouth. The swirl of his tongue and his gentle nibbles make my knees buckle.

He flicks his eyes up at me and hooks his fingers under the hem of my shorts and the elastic string of my underwear, pulling them both down.

I'm panting when he stands back upright and cups the back of my thighs, lifting me up onto the island.

"Ah," I cry out and smack his chest as the cold marble hits my skin.

He laughs and kisses me again. When he pulls away, his forehead is still touching mine while his hands squeeze my thighs. "Open your legs for me."

I inhale sharply and do as I was told.

Baylor takes a small step back and slides a thumb across my slippery core. His head tilts down to watch, and he licks his lower lip. "What, are you shy? Wider, Penny."

I push the outside of my knees against the counter, hovering on the edge.

"Good girl." He holds my gaze, and he kneels, sinking his mouth onto my center.

As soon as his tongue strokes my clit, I fall back onto my elbows and gasp. "Oh my God, Baylor."

His hot breath hits me as he releases a husky laugh. "You have no idea how long I've waited to make you say that with my tongue on your pussy."

My skin ignites at his words, and my thighs tremble as he hooks them over his shoulders, kissing me once again. His tongue works in skillful strokes. Swirling, sucking, and nibbling until I'm writhing beneath him. I thread my fingers through his hair, needing more.

He hums at my eagerness and grabs my thighs, yanking me further into him. I yipe as my entire ass leaves the counter.

He's holding me, devouring me.

My breath quickens as my core twists with a pending release, but Baylor rises before I find it.

I whimper, on the verge of tears.

In one swift movement, he pulls the elastic band of his briefs down and releases his cock. It hits my thigh before he grabs hold of it, and I almost reconsider what we're about to do because there's no way he'll fit.

Baylor's face pinches as he lines himself up at my entrance. "Fuck."

I squirm impatiently. "Baylor!"

"Stop. I don't have a condom," he rasps, taking a slow breath.

"You didn't plan on fucking me in the kitchen at four a.m.?" I giggle.

"No, smart-ass. But that's not going to stop me. Wrap your legs around me. I'm taking you upstairs."

I roll my hips forward and take the tip of him inside me. "Oops."

His possessive grip tightens. "Aspen. Fuck. Don't."

"It's okay. I'm on the pill."

His fingers dig into my hips as he thrusts himself all the way inside. "Why didn't you say that?"

I let out a small cry as my body stretches to fit him.

He pulls himself almost all the way out and thrusts into me again, pausing to give me time to adjust. "Look at me, Aspen. I want to see you."

I raise myself onto my hands and look up at him through hooded eyes. The way his gaze latches on to mine is both wild and all-consuming. I've never felt more wanted or desired—not just for my body, but for *me*. I want to drown in the sensation.

He leans over and kisses me, working his hips into a steadier rhythm.

I do my best to meet him as I drive my hips forward, taking his full length each time.

He lifts one of my bent knees higher, and his pumps become more uncontrolled.

My nerves are firing as the warmth builds again. I open my mouth in a silent plea, and Baylor drives into me harder. Faster. Grunting with each frantic movement.

I clench around him, my muscles fluttering.

"You're so fucking perfect," he says, breathing hard.

Rough fingers circle my clit only once, and my body trembles with its release. I implode, and his hand rushes to cover my mouth and silence my cries. I pinch my eyes shut as I ride it through to the end, seeing stars explode like fireworks behind my eyelids. I feel him swell inside me a second later and do the same for him, not letting a single grunt or moan leave his lips.

He kisses my hand tenderly to let me know when it's okay to remove it and then slowly lowers me back onto my feet.

I hold his arms for support and trail kisses up his chest until I reach his lips.

He smiles, breathless. "Fuck. You must really hate me, huh?"

I lift my chin, fighting a grin and failing. "More than ever."

He hums, bringing his lips to my forehead. "That's what I thought."

# 10

# CHRISTMAS MORNING

My warm pillow stirs beneath me, and I rub my eyes, trying to clear my vision so I can see what time it is. It's bright out, but I still feel like I could sleep another eight hours.

Rolling over, I reach for my phone on the side of the bed and feel the ache in my muscles.

My phone's not there.

Because this isn't my room.

I peek over at Baylor and see that he's already awake. Tousled hair, suckable lips, and bare chest. I wish I had a camera on me to capture such a perfect image and keep it forever.

"Hi," I say because I'm at a loss for words. What do you say when you wake up next to the last person you ever thought you'd wake up next to after he fucked you three—no, four—different ways?

A grin stretches across his face. "Mornin'."

I sit upright, looking at the mangled bedding. "What time is it?"

"Almost noon."

"Noon? Everyone must be downstairs, waiting for us!"

"Most likely."

"Baylor! How long have you been awake?"

"Couple of hours." He shrugs.

"You should've woken me up!"

I go to get off the bed, but he grabs my arms and pulls me back.

"What's the hurry?"

"I have to get dressed. They're going to know we're in here together."

"They probably already do. You weren't exactly quiet once I brought you up here."

Heat rises in my cheeks as the memories of just a few hours ago flood my mind. I don't remember the noises I made, but I wasn't exactly trying to stifle them anymore. "Oh God."

He props himself on his forearm. "Yeah, that's what you kept screaming."

I fist the pillow at my side and swing it at his face.

He twists his lips and narrows his eyes at me. "You wanna play this game with me?"

I giggle and fluff my pillow like I'm cocking a gun.

He launches himself forward on top of me before I can even get a second swing in and pins me to the mattress. A jolt of excitement flashes through me, which is quickly replaced with a surrendering cry as his hands poke my sides.

His eyes light up when he discovers how ticklish I am, and his hands attack as I wiggle beneath him helplessly. When I manage to get an arm free, I tickle his underarms.

*Oh-ho. The tables have turned.*

He stiffens and falls to the side, bringing me with him. We lie there for a moment, staring at each other, catching our breath as our laughter fades into silence. He has his hands collapsed around my wrists for good measure, but I kind of enjoy the strong hold he has on me.

I search his features, my mind suddenly racing with a million different questions.

He raises a dark brow. "Oh no. You've got that look."

"What look?" I frown.

"The overthinking one. I suppose it's well overdue." He finds my hand in the covers between us.

I glance down as we interlock fingers. "Why were you so horrible to me if you felt this way?"

He sighs like he's been dreading answering the unavoidable question. "Pushing you away from me was just an easier way of dealing with my feelings for you when I knew I couldn't act on them. And I think not being able to act on them made me angrier, and I usually aimed that at you." He reaches up and runs his thumb along my lower lip. "I'm sorry."

"What do you mean, you couldn't act on it? Why?"

"It's not really my place to say, but I don't really see any way around it at this point."

I wait for him to answer.

"Henry."

My brows shoot up. "Oh, come on. I know he tells you guys all the time to leave me alone, but I didn't think you were actually scared of him. It's not like he'd really do anything."

He shakes his head. "You're really that unaware?"

"What?"

"Henry has had a thing for you since the two of you met."

I look at him and tilt my head in confusion. "That's impossible. No way."

"Aspen, he missed out on front row seats the night the Rangers almost won the Stanley Cup, so he could help you with homework." He gives me a look.

"Well, it doesn't sound like he missed anything. It's not like they *won*," I tease, shaking my head. "He never told me that."

"You know how many times he's ditched us to hang out with you?"

I huff. "That proves nothing. I'm better company."

He smiles. "What is it with girls overlooking their guy friends? Most of them, if not all of them, want to sleep with you."

I scrunch my face. "Ew. He's like a brother."

"That's exactly why he's never told you."

I chew on my lip. *This is absurd.*

"Why do you think Henry invited us all out here for Christmas break?"

I frown. "He said Luke was going to be all alone, and then you and Jesse just kind of tagged along …"

Baylor laughs. "Luke hates his dad. He always spends the holidays alone; he likes it that way. Henry practically begged the three of us to come out, so it wouldn't be just you and him."

"We've been alone before."

"Yeah, but not for two weeks in a warm cabin with a scenic view of the mountains. It would've been torture."

My face falls. This makes no sense. All of the movie nights in Henry's apartment, the study sessions at our favorite coffee shop, searching for the perfect Chinese restaurant, the morning walks into school—none of those moments were romantic to me. There were no longing looks, no touching or flirting. Not once did I feel like Henry thought of me as anything more than a friend.

I rub my eyes, trying to relieve some of the pressure building into a headache. I feel stupid. Confused. Even slightly betrayed. Friends are supposed to be honest. But at the same time, I'm kind of glad I didn't know.

"This is a lot," I finally tell Baylor.

"I know." He clears his throat. "And I understand if you need time to think about you and me. I've felt this way for a long time, but this is all new to you."

I nod.

Baylor eyes me. "Do you regret this?"

I watch as he waves a finger between our bodies, and my chest warms. "If I thought it was a mistake, I wouldn't have made it so many times."

The way he smiles at me makes my stomach flutter. I'm so used to seeing him scowl and grimace at me. I like seeing this side of him—the happy side—and knowing I'm the cause of it.

"What made you suddenly change your mind and tell me?" I ask.

He turns and moves closer. "It was the way your body reacted to me when I found you naked."

I roll my eyes. "I was trying to get a rise out of you."

"And you liked it when you did."

I suck in a breath as he grabs my leg and wraps it around him.

"I saw it in your eyes. Your body language. That gave me hope. Henry had his chance. He's had two years to tell you how he feels about you, but he hasn't. I stayed away out of respect because he's my friend, but I'm done waiting. I'm done pretending. You deserve to be loved by someone who's not afraid to tell you how much you matter to them."

*Love? Did he say love?*

A small voice in my head is telling me to run, but an even louder voice is screaming at me to climb into his arms and never leave.

I listen to that one instead.

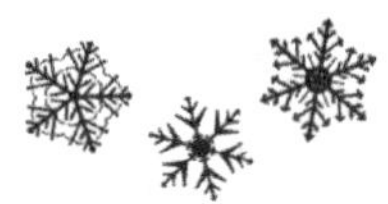

It's been two hours, and I finally have clothes on. My feet still hurt from the heels I wore last night, so I throw on some slippers to go with the rest of my comfy attire. All I plan on doing the rest of the day is eating and watching Christmas movies, if I can first survive the chaos that is coming when we leave our room.

No one's come searching for us, so it's safe to assume we've been found out. I think that's why I was okay with staying in bed longer. That, and Baylor's skilled fingers.

"Ready, beautiful?" Baylor asks, adjusting his collar.

"No."

He tilts my chin up to kiss me, sending me a new wave of confidence.

"Yes."

Whatever Marta's cooking wafts up into the bedroom, making my stomach growl.

"Let's go get something to eat. We've certainly worked up an appetite."

I giggle and follow him downstairs. Marta's in the kitchen. She gives us a big smile and a wave as we pass by, searching for the others. Before we even reach the bottom steps to the lower level, I hear whistling.

"Aye! Merry fucking Christmas to you two lovebirds!" Jesse stands up on a barstool, clapping.

"Finally come up for air, did you, B?" Luke claps a hand on Baylor's shoulder.

"This really is a gift to us all. It's about fucking time." Jesse beams. He's wearing a bedazzled red Santa hat I'm pretty sure belongs to Clara.

I laugh to hide the mortification bursting out of me.

Baylor does his best to ignore the attention and gets me a bottle of water from behind the bar, watching me to gauge how I'm handling this.

I offer him a smile before taking a long pull from my water. My hands are almost shaking as I twist the cap back on and steal a peek at Henry.

He's chalking up a pool cue on the other side of the pool table. He gives me a soft smile before leaning over and taking a shot.

Jesse walks over to me, looking pained. "You know, you kind of broke my heart with this one, Aspen. I propose to you, and you take another man to bed? I don't know if I'll ever recover."

"I'll still have you, Aspen." Luke winks. "You know I don't mind sharing."

Baylor swings a swift fist into Luke's stomach, and he keels over.

"Ah, man. It was a joke!" Luke protests.

While Jesse laughs at his friend's pain, I steal another glance at Henry. He's focused on lining up his next shot for practice, but I know he hasn't come over for a reason.

Nerves crawl up my spine, and my heart beats faster as I make my way over to him. "Merry Christmas, Henry."

He taps the cue ball but misses. "Merry Christmas, Pen."

"Can I talk to you for a minute?" I gesture to the other room.

He lays the pool stick on the table and follows me away from everyone else.

"Is something the matter?" he asks when we reach a quieter spot.

My fingernails dig into my palms. "I don't want you to be upset with me."

He pulls his brows in. "Why would I be—"

"Or Baylor," I add.

He stares at me, trying to decipher the look on my face. "I only ever told them to stay away from you because I thought that was what you wanted. You can make your own choices, Pen. I'm not here to stop you."

"He told me." There's a heaviness that comes after those words. I take a deep breath and continue, "Baylor said that you, um …" I push my fingers through my hair anxiously. "He told me how you … sort of …"

His eyes close when he realizes what I'm struggling to get out. "Shit."

"I didn't know you felt that way about me."

"That was kind of the whole point."

"I'm sorry, Henry."

He grips the back of the chair he's leaning on. "Please don't apologize."

"I just feel bad for not recognizing it." I shake my head. "I mean, I've seen you with girls, and that's completely different."

"None of the girls I've been with are girls I've ever seen a future with."

Guilt creeps up my throat, creating one big lump. "How come you never said anything?"

That question makes him sigh heavily. "Would it have made a difference?"

I look down.

"Exactly," he says. "It would've ruined everything. I know you, Pen. And I know that I'm not the type of guy you fall for."

"And why not?"

"Because you've dated guys just like me and it never works out. I told you, you need to find someone who challenges you."

We both drift our focus into the other room and look at Baylor.

"Now, that, I did not see coming."

I tuck a piece of hair behind my ear, watching as Baylor walks around the pool table, eyeing his lineup. He rolls his cuffs up and bends over, shooting a striped ball into the corner pocket.

Henry laughs once. "But, fuck, it kind of makes sense."

A smile tugs at my lips. "It does, doesn't it?"

The heaviness becomes more bearable, but I can't help but feel a sadness that our friendship will forever be changed. Different.

"Stop looking at me like I'm some sad puppy no one wants at the shelter. I'll find my girl someday, but I can't ever lose you as my friend, Aspen. I won't." His words are final.

My eyes burn, tears threatening to surface. "Okay," I say.

And then he hugs me, the same way he always has, and I feel like everything is going to be okay.

"Hey, Aspen. How does it feel to be one hundred grand richer?" Luke asks when I saunter back in.

"What?" I come to a halt in the middle of the room.

Henry points over at a stack of bills sitting on the poker table in the corner. "Your winnings."

I laugh.

"What's so funny?" Baylor asks.

"I'm not keeping that. I played with Henry's money. That's all his."

Henry shakes his head. "I took the money out that I'd put in for you to start with. The rest you won fair and square."

I look at Henry. "I beat those pricks for you."

"I know you did." He nods. "But I also think you did it for yourself."

I shake my head stubbornly. "Well, consider it a Christmas gift."

"Since when do we exchange gifts, Pen?" Henry asks with a smirk on his face.

"Whatever. Then, it's for inviting me out here. I don't want it."

"Take it, Aspen," Baylor insists. "Use it to pay off school, and for fuck's sake, get yourself out of that dorm of yours."

"I'll take it," Jesse offers.

Both Baylor and Henry shoot him a look of annoyance.

"This isn't a handout, Pen. There are no strings that come with it, okay? It's yours." Henry tries to reassure me. "Taking it doesn't make you like your dad."

I swallow hard, hating that I'm finding less reasons not to take it. "Fine. Maybe."

They erupt in cheers.

"One of us! One of us!" Jesse calls out as he pours us all glasses of champagne.

I take a sip after we all toast and wander over to the pool table with Baylor.

His fingers skim down my arm as he holds out a pool cue. "Wanna play a game?"

I set my glass down, grinning.

Baylor stares at me intently. "What are you up to?"

"Anyone up for a game of eight-ball doubles? I think it's only fair I let you boys try and win some of your money back."

"Absolutely." Jesse nods.

"Fuck yeah," Luke says.

Luke and Jesse hop off their stools, giving each other high fives.

"Looks like you're stuck with me as your partner." I look up at Baylor.

"Sounds good to me, baby." He leans down, giving me a wicked grin, and then plants a soft kiss on my lips.

"I've never played before. Do you think you guys can teach me the rules?" I pull away and eye the three of them while chalking up my cue.

Luke and Jesse trade glances with each other and then look back at Henry, who's watching from the bar with pure amusement. They turn back around just in time to see me break and let out a string of curse words.

# 11

# A PRESENT FOR PENNY

A large black gift bag is sitting on my bed when I return with my fresh laundry. I hate bringing home dirty clothes after a trip, so when I get the opportunity, I wash them right before I leave. I hate that it's already time to go. The days following Christmas have been a delicious, toe-curling blur. It's hard to believe that, two weeks ago, I was packing my bags for this trip, blindly unaware of what it was going to turn out to be for me. I came here, hating Baylor Frost, and I'm leaving with the certainty that we are a perfect match.

Two weeks. That's all it took.

I throw my clothes into a pile on the bed, eyeing the mysterious bag as if it might reveal itself to me without my having to open it. I reach for the small white tag hanging from the handle and read my name written across it.

Baylor comes out of the bathroom, brushing his teeth with just a towel around his waist. "That's for you," he says with a mouthful of toothpaste.

"I see that. What for?"

"Late Christmas present." He shrugs.

"Baylor"—I frown—"I didn't know we were doing gifts. I didn't get you anything."

His eyes crease with a smile. "You gave me the one thing no one else could. You."

My chest tightens.

"Just open it already."

I flick my eyes down at his towel. "You? Or this bag?"

He shakes his head and goes back into the bathroom to rinse his mouth out. When he returns, he pulls the tissue paper out from inside the bag and hands me the smaller bag inside of it. I've never known Baylor to be a patient man.

"When did you do this?" I ask, smiling.

"I drove into town with Henry when you were cooking the other night. I went and picked it up this morning while you were still sleeping. Sorry it's late. The man said it would take a couple of days."

My lips pinch as I take it from him.

"It's not like I bought you a car." He laughs.

"I just hate not having something for you to unwrap." I pout.

"What do you think I did Christmas morning on Henry's kitchen island?" he taunts. "Your gift kept on giving. And giving. And—"

I cut him off with a light smack to the chest.

He smiles and nods at the present. "Go on."

I pull a soft leather bag out from the fabric encasing it and hold it by its handle. My fingers run across the maroon stitching in the front that reads, *Penny*.

"This is beautiful, Baylor," I say, looking up at him.

His face softens. "When we were headed up the mountain in the gondola ride before you went and sprained your wrist, it was your first time really seeing this place. Your face …" A smile touches his lips at the memory. "Words can't describe the way it felt to see you light up the way you did."

I remember the moment, but I thought he was laughing at me.

"I decided I wanted to be able to experience that with you in every new place you visit. I want to travel with you to Greece, Japan, Spain—anywhere that will give you that same look of amazement when you see it for the first time."

Tears spring to my eyes, and I swallow the overwhelming emotion rippling through me. Once again, I'm struck by the contradiction of the cold and hateful Baylor I thought I knew, and the warm and thoughtful Baylor I can't seem to get enough of now. Maybe there really is a thin line between love and hate. If there is, Baylor and I walked that line like a tightrope for the last two years. He was just waiting for me to fall with him.

"This"—he points to the bag with my name on it—"is so you have something better to pack your things in. I'm not traveling with you if you bring that hideous duffel with you when we go."

"Baylor!" I squeal, dropping my mouth open. I glance around the room for my bag. I thought I left it beside the bed. "Wait, where is it? Where's my duffel?"

He closes his arms around me, brushing his lips against mine. "I have no idea," he says, feigning ignorance. "It's a complete mystery really."

"You're despicable." I smile up at him, curling into the warmth of his embrace.

"Yeah?" Baylor leans into my ear and whispers, "Tell me how much you hate me."

# ABOUT THE AUTHOR

N.J. Gray was born and raised in Minnesota, but she is currently exploring the Rocky Mountains with her husband and two rescue dogs, Jango and Korra. She loves to indulge herself in hard-fought romance novels and considers herself an enthusiast of all things sweet. She writes from her home in Colorado Springs, Colorado.

Please visit her at www.authornjgray.com or www.instagram.com/thenjgray.

Made in the USA
Monee, IL
02 August 2023

40320329R00080